WALTER AND THE WIRELESS

Also by Sara Ware Bassett

<table>
<tr><td>

THE YOUNG ENGINEERS

Carl and the Cotton Gin
Christopher and the
    Clockmakers
Paul and the Printing Press
Steve and the Steam Engine
Ted and the Telephone
Walter and the Wireless

</td><td>

THE STORY OF

The Story of Glass
The Story of Leather
The Story of Silk
The Story of Sugar
The Story of Porcelain
The Story of Lumber
The Story of Wool

</td></tr>
</table>

This edition published 2026
by Living Book Press
Copyright © Living Book Press, 2026

ISBN: 978-1-76153-454-6 (hardcover)
          978-1-76153-456-0 (softcover)

First published in 1923.

This edition is based on the Little, Brown, and Company printing by 1923.

A catalogue record for this book is available from the National Library of Australia

WALTER AND THE WIRELESS

by

SARA WARE BASSETT

"K Y W Chicago, Illinois. Stand by fifteen minutes for———."

Contents

CHAPTER I

HIS HIGHNESS

His Highness came by the nickname honestly enough and yet those who heard it for the first time had difficulty in repressing a smile at the incongruity of the title. In fact perhaps no term could have been found that would have been less appropriate. For Walter King possessed neither dignity of rank nor of stature. On the contrary he was a short, snub-nosed boy of fifteen, the epitome of good humor and democracy.

His hair was red and towsled, his face spangled with great golden freckles which sea winds and sunshine had multiplied until there was scarce room for another on his beaming countenance. Hands and arms were freckled too, for when one lives in a bathing suit six months of the year and is either in the water or on it most of the time the skin fails to retain its pristine whiteness of hue. But His Highness did not care a fig for that. He was far too busy baiting eel and lobster traps, mending fish nets, untangling lines, and painting boats to give a thought to his personal beauty.

Indeed his mother often bewailed the fact that he was not more interested in his appearance and there were times when it seemed as if she were right. Certainly when her son ambled home at dusk with every rebellious hair standing upended upon his head and a string of flounders dripping salt from the tips of their slimy tails she was justified to a degree in wishing he had more regard for the niceties of life.

"Look at the mess you're making!" she would pipe indignantly. "I've just mopped this floor, Walter."

"You have? Now isn't that the dickens! Well, no matter, Ma; I'll swab the place down again when I've finished cleaning these fish. They're beauties, aren't they? A batch of them fried won't go bad for supper to-night. I'm hungry as a bear. Shouldn't think I'd eaten anything in ten years. Say, Ma, what do you s'pose? Dave Corbett was out in the *Nancy* three hours and never got a bite. What do you think of that? The wind died down, his engine got stalled, and he and Hosey Talbot had to row home from the Bell Reef Shoals. Haw, haw! Maybe I didn't roar when I saw them come pulling in against the tide, mad as two man-eating sharks. Fit to harpoon the first person they met, they were. I sung out and asked them were they practicing for the Harvard and Yale boat race and Dave was that peeved he shied an oarlock after me. Haw, haw, haw!"

"You ought not to provoke Dave, Walter."

"Provoke him? But he was provoked already, Ma. There's no harm putting an extra stick on the fire when it's burning, anyhow. Besides, Dave is never in earnest when he bawls me out. He just likes to hear himself scold."

"He has a terrible temper."

"Oh, I know half the town is scart to death of him. But he always will take a jolly from me. We understand each other, Dave and I. Say, Ma, these rubber boots leak. Did you know that? Yes, siree! They leak like sieves. I might as well be without 'em."

Mrs. King sighed.

"I don't see," murmured she, "how you manage to go through

everything you have so quickly, Walter. Nothing you wear lasts you more than a week."

"Oh, I say, make it a month. Do, now!"

He saw his mother smile faintly.

"Well, a month then."

"You couldn't stretch it to two?"

"Not possibly. Four weeks seems to be your limit."

The sharpness of her tone, however, had weakened.

"Four weeks, eh? I did think I'd had these rubber boots longer than that. It is amazing how attached you can get to things even in a little while."

Holding aloft the knife with which he was preparing to behead the unlucky flounders, His Highness gazed reflectively down at his feet.

"It's awful that I have to keep having so many things, isn't it? I hate to be costing you money all the time. Now if you'd only let me ship for the Grand Banks when the *Katie B.* goes out——"

"Walter! What is the use of digging up that old bone again? I never shall let you ship for the Grand Banks or any other Banks so long as I live. We've had this out hundreds of times before. You know you and Bob are all I've got in the world. Do you suppose I want you lost in a fog and never heard from again?"

"Oh, Great Scott, Ma! They don't lose fishing boats now as they used to. They carry wireless, and the fleet keeps in touch every minute."

"The dories have no wireless aboard them," observed Mrs. King grimly.

"I suppose not, no, probably they don't," His Highness admitted reluctantly.

"Anyway, wireless or no wireless, you are not going on a fishing cruise to the Grand Banks."

"I hear you, Ma," grinned the boy.

"There is plenty of work right here on the land if you're looking for it. Why must you always be wanting to go to sea to earn money?"

"Faith, Mother, I don't know," laughed Walter. "I expect it's because I see chores to do when I'm afloat that I can't see ashore. It is the way I was born."

"A poor way."

"Maybe it is. At any rate I can't help it."

"I'm afraid you do not try to help it very hard."

The lad shrugged his shoulders.

"There's that chance you have to hire out at the Crownin-shields' for the summer."

"Those snobs."

"Beggars cannot be choosers. Besides, they may not be snobs at all. What makes you think they are?"

"Oh, I don't mind the lugs they put on," protested Walter, evading the issue. "I suppose all New York swells do that. It's what they want me for that gets my goat." Again the knife he held was tragically upraised. "How would you like to be nursemaid to six or eight brainless little pups no bigger than rats? Not but what I like dogs. I'd like nothing better than to own a fine dog of some spirit. But those imitations! Why, before a week was out, I'd have their necks wrung."

"Mr. Crowninshield promised to pay you well."

"What's money if all the kids in town are going to josh you?"

"Money is a good deal when you need it." His mother shook her head gravely. "Have you ever considered how badly we are in want of money, Walter?"

"What do you mean, Ma?" The boy wheeled about, startled.

"I haven't said anything about it, dear, because I could not bear to have you boys bothered," was the quiet answer. "But lately things have not been going well and I have been pretty much worried. The money your Uncle Henry invested for us isn't paying any dividends; there seems to be something the matter with the company's affairs. As for your Uncle Mark Miller, I've heard nothing from him in months. His ship was to put in at Shanghai for cargo and I ought to have had a letter by now; but none has come and I am afraid something must be the trouble. He is a good brother and never fails to send me money. I can ill afford to be without help now when the mortgage is coming due and I have so many bills to meet. It takes a deal of money to live nowadays. You boys do not realize that."

"Why, I had no idea you were fussed, Mother, and I'm sure Bob hadn't either," declared Walter soberly.

"Then I have done better than I thought I had," returned his mother, with the shadow of a smile. "I wanted to keep it secret if I could."

"But you shouldn't have tried to keep it a secret, Mater dear," Walter replied. "I'm sure we'd rather know—at least I would."

"But what use is it?"

"Use? Why, all the use in the world, Ma. I shall go ahead and take Mr. Crowninshield's job for one thing."

"But you said——"

"Shucks! I was only fooling about the dogs, Mother. I shan't really mind exercising and taking care of them at all. Of course, I won't deny I'd rather they were Great Danes or police dogs; I'd even prefer Airedales or Cockers. Still I suppose these little mopsey Pekingese must have some brains or the Lord would not have made them. No doubt I shall get used to them in time."

"It is only for the summer vacation anyway, you know,"

ventured his mother. "The Crowninshields go back to New York in October."

"I certainly ought to be able to bear up a few months," laughed Walter, with a ludicrously wry twist of his mouth. "I hate to think you've been bothered and have been keeping it all to yourself."

"Misery does like company," Mrs. King returned with an unsteady laugh. "I believe I feel better already for having told you. But you must not worry, dear. We shall pull through all right, I guess. How I came to speak of it I don't know. It was only that it seemed such a pity to toss the Crowninshield offer aside without even considering it. Nobody knows where it might end. The village people say Mr. Crowninshield is a very generous man, especially if he takes a fancy to anybody."

"But he may not take a fancy to me."

"He must have done so already to be asking you to help with the dogs."

"Nonsense, Ma! Did you think Mr. Crowninshield picked me out himself? Why, he's never laid eyes on me. That great privilege is still in store for him. No, he simply told Jerry Thomas, the caretaker, to find somebody for the job before the family arrived. He doesn't care a darn who it is so long as he has a person who can be trusted with his priceless pups. Why, I heard the other day that a dealer from New York had offered five thousand dollars for the smallest one."

"Walter!"

"Straight goods!"

"Five thousand dollars for a dog!" gasped Mrs. King.

Her son chuckled at her incredulity.

"Sure!"

"But it's a fortune," murmured she. "I had no idea there was a dog on earth worth that much."

"All of them are not."

"But five thousand dollars!" she repeated. "Why, Walter, I wouldn't have you responsible for a creature like that for anything in the world. You might as well attempt to be custodian of a lot of gold bonds. I shouldn't have a happy moment or sleep a wink thinking of it. Suppose some of the little wretches were to run away and get lost? Or suppose they were to be stolen? Or they might get sick and die on your hands."

"That is why they want a responsible person to keep an eye on them."

His Highness squared his shoulders and threw out his chest.

"But you are not a responsible person," burst out Mrs. King with unflattering candor.

"Mother!"

"Well—are you?" she insisted.

The boy's figure shriveled.

"No," he confessed frankly, "I'm afraid I'm not."

"Of course you're not," continued his mother with the same brutal truthfulness. "It isn't that you do not mean to be, sonny," added she kindly. "But your mind wanders off on all sorts of things instead of the thing you're doing. That is why you do not get on better in school. All your teachers say you are bright enough if you only had some concentration to back it up. What you can be thinking of all the time I cannot imagine; but certainly it isn't your lessons."

"I know," nodded Walter without resentment. "My mind does flop about like a kite. I think of everything but what I ought to. It's a rotten habit."

"Well, all I can say is you'd be an almighty poor one to look after a lot of valuable dogs," sniffed his mother.

"I'll bet I could do it if I set out to."

"But would you set out to—that is the question? Would you really put your entire attention on those dogs so that other people could drop them from their minds? That is what taking care means."

"I couldn't promise. I could only try."

"I should never dare to have you undertake it."

"That settles it, Ma," announced His Highness. "I've evidently got to prove to you that you are wrong. I'm going up to Crowninshields' this minute to tell Jerry he can count on me from July until October."

"You're crazy."

"Wait and see."

"I know what I'll see," was the sharp retort. "I shall see all those puppies kicking up their heels and racing off to Provincetown, and Mr. Crowninshield insisting that you either find them and bring them back or pay him what they cost him."

"Don't you believe it."

"That is what will happen," was the solemn prophecy.

"But you were keen for me to take the job."

"That was before I knew what the little rats were worth."

"You just thought it was a cheap sort of a position and that I was to race round and make it pleasant for a lot of ordinary curs, didn't you?" interrogated the lad with mock indignation.

In spite of herself his mother smiled.

"Well, you see you were wrong," went on Walter. "It is not that sort of thing at all. It is a job for a trustworthy man, Jerry Thomas said, and will bring in good wages."

"It ought to," replied his mother sarcastically, "if a person must spend every day for three months sitting with his eyes glued on those mites watching every breath they draw."

"It isn't just days, Mother; I'd have to be there nights as well."

"What!"

"That's what Jerry told me. I'd have to sleep on the place. Mr. Crowninshield wants some one there all the time."

"But Walter——!" Mrs. King broke off in dismay.

"I know that would mean leaving you alone now that Bob has a regular position at the Seaver Bay Wireless station. Still, why should you mind? I have always been gone all day, anyhow; and at night I sleep so soundly that you yourself have often said burglars might carry away the bed from under me and I not know it."

"You are not much protection, that's a fact," confessed Mrs. King. "Fortunately, though, I am not a timid person. It is not that I am afraid to stay here alone. My chief objection is that it seems foolish to run a great house like this simply for myself."

"Couldn't you get some one to come and keep you company?"

"Who, I should like to know?"

"Why—why—well, I haven't thought about it. Of course there's Aunt Marcia King."

"Mercy on us!" exclaimed his mother, instantly flaring up. "I'd rather see the evil one himself put in an appearance than your Aunt Marcia. Of all the fault-finding, critical, sharp-tongued creatures in the world she is the worst. Why, I'd let burglars carry away every stick and stone I possess and myself thrown in before I would ask her here to board."

"My, Mother! I'd no idea you had such a temper. You're as bad as Dave Corbett," asserted Walter teasingly.

His mother tossed her head but he saw her flush uncomfortably.

"I suppose you wouldn't want a regular boarder," suggested the boy in order to turn the conversation.

"A *boarder*!" There was less disapproval than surprise in the ejaculation, however.

"Lots of people in the town do take summer boarders," added he.

"The thought never entered my head before," reflected his mother aloud. "There certainly is plenty of room in the house, and we have a royal view of the water. Besides, there's the garden. Strangers are always coming here in vacation time and asking if they may look at it or sketch it. It never seemed anything very remarkable to me for most of the flowers have sown themselves and grow like weeds, but of course there's no denying the hollyhocks, poppies, and larkspur are pretty. But visitors always call it wonderful."

"Most likely you could get a big price if you were to rent rooms."

"I'm sure I could," replied Mrs. King thoughtfully. "It would help toward the mortgage and the other bills, too. I've half a mind to try it, Walter."

"It would mean extra work for you."

"Pooh! What do I care for that? Not a fig! In fact, with both of you boys away I'd rather be busy than not," was the quick retort.

"Do you suppose Bob would mind?"

"Bob? Why, he's seldom at home nowadays. Why should he care?"

"Aunt Marcia might think——" began the boy mischievously. But the comment was cut short.

"Oh, I know what your Aunt Marcia would say," broke in Mrs. King. "She'd hold up her hands in horror and announce that it was beneath the dignity of the family to take boarders."

They both laughed.

"I believe the very notion of scandalizing her will be what

will decide me," concluded his mother with finality. "I'll put an advertisement in the Boston paper to-morrow and see what luck I have. If the right people do not turn up, why I don't have to take them."

"Sure you don't."

"It's a good plan, a splendid plan, Walter. Boarders will give me company and money too. I wonder it never occurred to me to do it before." Then she patted the lad's shoulder, adding playfully, "I guess if you have brains in one direction you must have them in another. Still, as I said before, I do not fancy your being responsible for those dogs."

"Pooh! You quit worrying, Ma, or I shall be sorry I told you they were blue ribbon pups."

"I should have heard of it, never fear. You hear of everything in this town. You can't help it. Like as not everybody in the place will know by to-morrow morning that I am going to take boarders. Luckily I don't care—that's one good thing. And as to the dogs, if you are resolved to accept that position all I can say is that you must keep a head on your shoulders. You cannot hire out for a job unless you are prepared to give a full return for the money paid you. It is not honest. So think carefully what you mean to do before you embark. And remember, if you get into some careless scrape you cannot come back on me for money for I haven't any to hand over."

"I shall shoulder my own blame," responded Walter, drawing in his chin.

"Well and good then. If you are ready to do that, it is your affair and I have nothing more to say," announced Mrs. King, preparing to leave the room.

But Walter stayed her on the threshold.

"I don't see," he began, "why you always seem to expect I'm

going to get into a scrape. You are never looking for trouble with Bob."

"Bob! Bless your heart I never have to! You know that as well as I do. Any one could trust Bob until the Day of Judgment. He never forgets a word you tell him. Ask him to do an errand and it is as good as done. You can drop it from your mind. From a little child he was dependable like that. His teachers couldn't say enough about him. Wasn't he always at the head of his class? The way he's turned out is no surprise. Think of his picking up wireless enough outside school hours to get a radio job during the war, and afterward that fine position at Seaver Bay! Few lads his age could have done it. And think of the messages he's entrusted with—government work, and sinking ships, and goodness knows what not!"

The proud mother ceased for lack of breath.

"I wish I was like Bob," sighed Walter gloomily.

"Nonsense!" was the instant exclamation. "You're yourself, and scatter-brain as you are, I'd want you no different. You're but a lad yet. When you are Bob's age you may be like him. Who knows?"

"I'm afraid not," came dismally from Walter. "I haven't started out as Bob did."

"What if you haven't? There's time enough to catch up if you hurry. And anyway, I do not want my children all alike. Variety is the spice of life. I wouldn't have you patterned after Bob if I could speak the word."

"You wouldn't?" the boy brightened.

"Indeed I wouldn't! Who would I be patching torn trousers or darning ripped sweaters for if you were like Bob, I'd like to know? Who'd be pestering me to hunt up his cap and mittens? And who would I be frying clams for?"

"Bob never could abide clam fritters, could he?" put in the younger brother.

"Bob never had any frivolities," mused Mrs. King, shaking her head. "Sometimes I've almost wished he had if only to keep the rest of us in countenance. Many's the time I've feared lest he was going to die he was that near perfect."

"Well, Ma, you haven't had to lie awake worrying because I was too good for this world, have you?" chuckled His Highness, breaking into a grin.

His mother regarded him affectionately.

"Oh, you'll make your way too, sonny, some day. It won't be as Bob has done it; but you'll make it nevertheless. Folks are going to do things for you simply because they cannot help it."

The boy studied her with a puzzled expression.

"What do you mean, Mater?"

As if coming out of a reverie Mrs. King started, the mistiness that had softened her eyes vanishing.

"There! Look at the way you've splashed up my nice clean sink!" complained she tartly. "Did any one ever see such a child— always messing up everything! Come, clear out of here and take your fish with you. It does seem as if you needed four nursemaids and a valet at your heels to pick up after you. Be off this minute."

With a cloth in one hand and a bar of soap in the other, she elbowed him away from the dishpan.

"You'll fry these flounders for supper, won't you, Ma?" called the lad as he disappeared into the shed.

"Fry 'em? I reckon I'll have to. It's wicked to catch fish and not use 'em."

But he saw his mother's eyes twinkle and her grumbling assent did not trouble him.

CHAPTER II

THE NEW JOB

May at Lovell's Harbor was one of the most beautiful seasons of the year. In fact the inhabitants of the town often remarked that they put up with the winters the small isolated village offered for the sake of its springs and summers. Certain it was that when easterly storms swept the marshes and lashed the harbor into foam; when every boat that struggled out of the channel returned whitened to the gunwale with ice, there was little to induce anybody to take up residence in the hamlet. How cold and blue the water looked! How the surf boomed up on the lonely beach and the winds howled and whined around the eaves of the low cottages!

One buttoned himself tightly into a greatcoat then, twisted a muffler many times about his neck, pulled his cap over his ears, and rushed for school with a velocity that almost equaled the scudding schooners whose sails billowed large against the horizon. At least that was what His Highness, Walter King, invariably did.

But from the instant the breath of spring stole into the air,— ah, then Lovell's Harbor became a different place altogether. The stems of the willows fringing the small fresh-water ponds mellowed to bronze before one's very eyes; the dull reaches of salt grass turned emerald; the steely tint of the sea softened to azure and glinted golden in the sun. How shrill sounded the cries of the redwings in the marsh! How jolly the frogs' twilight chorus!

The miracle went on with amazing rapidity. Soon you were scouring the hollows in the woods for arbutus or splashing bare-legged into the bogs for cowslips. You even ventured knee-deep into the sea which although still chill was no longer frigid. And then, before you knew it, you were hauling out your fishing tackle and looking over your flies; inspecting the old dory and calking her seams with a coat of fresh paint. Then came the raking of the leaves, the uncovering of the hollyhocks, and the burning of brush; and through the mists of smoke that rose high in the air you could hear the resonant chee-ee of the blackbirds swinging on the reeds along the margin of the creek.

And afterward, when summer had really made its appearance, what days of blue and gold followed! Was ever sky so cloudless, grass so vividly green, or ocean so sparkling? Ah, a boy never lacked amusement now! He wriggled into his bathing suit directly after breakfast and was off to the shore to swim, fish, or sail, or do any of the thousand-and-one alluring things that turned up. And things always did turn up in that small horseshoe where the boats made in. It was the club of Lovell's Harbor.

Here all the men of the village congregated daily to smoke, swap jokes, and heckle those who worked.

"That's no way to mend a net, Eph," one of the spectators would protest. "Where was you fetched up, man? Tote the durn thing over here and I'll show you how they do it off the Horn."

Or another member of the audience would call:

"Was you reckonin' you'd have enough paint in that keg to finish your yawl, Eddie? Never in the world! What are you so scrimpin' of it for? Slither it on good and thick and let it trickle down into the cracks. 'Twill keep 'em tight."

Oh, one learned to curb his temper and bend to the higher criticism if he carried his work down to the beach. He got an abundance of advice whether he asked for it or not and for the most part the counsel was sound and helpful. There you heard also tales of tempests, wrecks, strange ports, and sea serpents,— weird tales that chilled your blood; and sometimes the piping note of an old chanty was raised by one whose sailing days were now only a memory.

What marvel that to be a boy at Lovell's Harbor was a boon to be coveted even if along with the distinction went a throng of homely tasks such as shucking clams, cleaning cod, baiting lobster pots, and running errands? No cake is all frosting and no chowder all broth. You had to take the bad along with the good if you lived at Lovell's Harbor. And while you were sandwiching in work and fun what an education you got! Why, it was better than a dozen schools. Not only did you learn to swim like a spaniel, pull a strong oar, hoist a sail, and gain an understanding of winds and tides, but also you came to handle tools with an ease no manual training school could teach you. You made a wooden pin do if you had no nail; and a bit of rope serve if the whittled pin were lacking. Instead of hurrying to a shop to purchase new you patched up the old, and the triumph of doing it afforded a satisfaction very pleasant to experience.

Moreover, as a result, you had more pennies in your pocket and more brains in your head. Both Bob and Walter King, as well as most of the other village lads, outranked the town-bred boy in all-round practical skill. They may not have cut such a fine figure at golf or dancing; perhaps they did not excel at Latin or French; but they had at the tips of their tongues numberless useful facts which they had tried out and proven workable and which no city dweller could possibly have gleaned.

His Highness might be freckled and towsled and, as his mother affirmed, forgetful and careless, but like a sponge his active young mind had soaked up a deal no books could have given him. You would best beware how you jollied Walter King or put him down for a "Rube." More than likely you would later regret your snap judgment.

No doubt it was this realization that had stimulated Jerry Thomas to ask him to come to Surfside, the Crowninshields' big summer estate, and look after the dogs. Jerry was an old resident of Lovell's Harbor, and having watched the boy grow up, he unquestionably knew what he was about. That there were plenty of other boys at the Harbor to choose from was certain. If the honor descended to His Highness, rest assured it was not without reason.

Hence Jerry was not only pleased but immensely gratified when on the morning following Walter rounded the corner of the great barn and appeared in the doorway.

"I've come to say Yes to that job you offered me the other day," announced he, without wasting words on preliminaries.

"Good, youngster!"

"When shall you want me?"

"When can you come?" grinned Jerry.

He was a lank, sharp-featured man with china blue eyes that narrowed to a mere slit when he smiled, and from the corners of which crowsfeet, like fan-shaped streaks of light from the rising sun, radiated across his temples. His skin was tanned to the hue of old hickory and deep down in its furrows were lines of white. He had a big nose that was always sunburned, powerful hands with a reddish fuzz on their backs, and gnarled fingers that bore the scars of innumerable nautical disasters. But the chief glory he possessed was a neatly tattooed schooner that sailed under full canvas upon his forearm and bore beneath it the inscription:

The Mollie D. The finest ship afloat.

The words had been intended as a tribute rather than a challenge for Jerry was a peaceful soul, but unfortunately they had proved provocative of many a brawl, and had the truth been known a certain odd slant of Jerry's chin could have been traced back to this apparently harmless assertion. Possibly had this mate of the *Mollie D.* foreseen into what straits his boast was to lead him he might not have expressed it so baldly in all the naked glory of blue ink; but with the sentiment once immortalized what choice had he but to defend it? Therefore, being no coward but a sturdy seaman with a swinging undercut, he had in times past delivered many a blow in order to uphold the *Mollie D.'s* nautical reputation, after which encounters his challengers were wont to emerge with a more profound respect not only for the bark but for Jerry Thomas as well.

All that, however, was long ago. Since the great storm of 1890 when so many ships had perished and the *Mollie D.*, bound from Norfolk to Fairhaven, had gone down with the rest, Jerry had abandoned the sea. It was not the perils of the deep, nevertheless, that had driven him landward, or the fear of future disasters; it was only that since his first love was lost he could not bring himself to ship on any other vessel.

Accordingly he took to the shore and for a time a very strange misfit he was there. How he fumed and fidgeted and roamed from one place to another, searching for some spot in which his restless spirit would find peace! And then one day he had wandered into Lovell's Harbor and there he had stayed ever since. For several seasons he had taken out sailing parties of summer boarders or piloted amateur fishermen out to the

Ledges; but the timidity and lack of sophistication of these city patrons at length so rasped his nerves that he gave up the task and was about to betake himself to pastures new when he fell beneath the eye of Mr. Glenmore Archibald Crowninshield, a New York banker, who had bought the strip of land forming one arm of the bay and was on the point of erecting there a diminutive summer palace.

From that instant Jerry's fortune was made. Mr. Crowninshield was a keen student of human nature and was immediately attracted to the sailor with his ambling gait and twinkling blue eyes. Moreover, the New Yorker happened to be in search of just such a man to look out for his interests when he was not at Lovell's Harbor. Hence Jerry was elevated to the post of caretaker and delegated to keep guard over the edifice that was about to be erected.

In view of the fact that up to the moment Jerry had been the most care-free mortal alive and had never from day to day been able to remember the whereabouts of his sou'wester or his rubber boots, his ensuing transformation was nothing short of a miracle. Promptly settling down with doglike fidelity he began mildly to urge on the lagging carpenters; but presently, magnificent in his wrath, he rose above them, whiplash in hand, and drove them forward. His watery blue eyes followed every stick of timber, every foot of piping, every nail that was placed. There was no escaping his watchfulness. If corners were not true or moldings did not meet he saw and called attention to it. Many a time a slipshod workman was ready to throw him over the cliff into the sea and perhaps might have done so had he not been conscious of the justice of the criticism.

In consequence the Crowninshield house was built on honor; and when the bills began to come in and showed a marked falling off in magnitude the owner of the mansion could not but express gratitude. Jerry, however, did not covet thanks. Instead he tagged along at his employer's heels, proudly calling notice first to one skillful bit of work and then to another. The house and all that concerned it became his hobby. It was to him what the *Mollie D.* had been, the primary interest of his life. He knew every inch of plumbing; where every shut-off, valve, ventilator, and stopcock was located. Moreover, he could have told, had not his jaws been clamped together tightly as a scallop shell, exactly how much every article in the mansion cost.

Later he superintended the grading of the lawns, the laying out of tennis courts, and the building of garages, boathouses, and bathhouses. By this time Mr. Crowninshield would willingly have trusted him with every farthing he possessed so complete was his confidence in his man Friday.

Jerry, however, was modest. He declared he had only done his duty and insisted that it go at that. But having set this high standard of fidelity for himself it followed that he demanded a like faithfulness in others; and if he were not merciful to those who came under his dictatorship at least no one of them could deny that he was just. Hence Walter King did not shrink from the prospect of working with him, stern though he was reputed to be. One can only do one's best and that the boy was determined to do. Therefore he smiled up into Jerry's misty blue eyes and answered:

"I could begin work when school closes toward the end of June."

"Humph! I wish you could make it earlier. Well, we must put up with that since it is the best you can do. Goodness knows I'd be the last one to discourage learning in the young. I got all too little of it when I was a shaver. Not a day goes by that I don't wish I'd had my chance. I shipped to sea when I was only twelve—would go—nothing would stop me—and I've been knocking round ever since, picking up here and there what scraps of knowledge I could get. Don't let anything tempt you to sea till you're full-grown, sonny, for you'll live to regret it, sure as my name is Jerry Taylor."

Walter flushed guiltily, wondering as he did so whether Jerry's little blue eyes had bored their way into his skull and read there his aspirations.

"Nope!" went on the sailor. "Take it from me, seafaring is a man's job. You much better stay ashore and——" he stopped as if at a loss and then smiling broadly added, "play governess to a pack of dogs."

"I figure that is about what I'm going to do," replied His Highness with a comic air of resignation.

"Well, what's the matter with that?" inquired Jerry sharply. "You'll be getting paid for it, won't you—well paid? And you'll have cozy quarters all to yourself, and three good meals a day. Land alive! Some folks want the earth! Why, when I was your age, I was swung up in a hammock between decks with not an inch of space that I could call my own. If I wanted to stow away anything I hadn't a place to put it where it wasn't common property. As for meals I took what I could get and was thankful that I didn't starve. And here you come along and tilt up your freckled pug nose at a room and board and ten a week. Bah! What's come over this generation anyway?"

"I wasn't turning up my nose," Walter ventured to protest. "It turns up anyhow."

"Then you need to be careful how you make it go higher," grinned Jerry.

"And—and—I had no idea you meant to pay me that much."

"What do you think we are up here?" bristled Jerry. "A sweatshop? No siree! We stand for the square deal every time, we do. Only you've got to understand, young one, that it's to be square on both sides. You're to do no shirking; if you do you'll get fired so quick you'll wonder what hit you. But if you do your part you need have no worries. Now think good and plenty before you embark on the cruise."

"I have thought."

"All right then. We'll haul up anchor and be off the latter part of June."

"You'll have to tell me exactly what you want me to do."

"Oh, I'll tell you right 'nough," drawled Jerry, with a humorous twist of his lips. "You'll get a chart to sail by. Still, it won't wholly cover your duties. The thing for you to do is to keep your eyes peeled and look alive. Watch out and see where there's a hole an' be in that hole so it won't be empty. That's the best recipe I know for being useful."

"I'll try."

"If you honestly do that I reckon there'll be no cause for you to worry," observed the caretaker kindly. "Towards the end of June, then, I'll be on the lookout for you. Your quarters will be all ready, shipshape and trim as a liner's cabin."

"Where will they be?" inquired Walter.

"Want to see 'em?"

"I'd like to, yes."

"I s'pose you would," nodded Jerry. "You can as well as not; only they ain't fixed up as they'll be later. Look kinder dismal."

"Oh, I shan't mind."

The big man smiled at the eagerness of the boy's tone.

"Likely you ain't never been away from home before, son," said he, as he took a key out of a glass case on the wall of the barn and slipped it into his pocket.

"No—that is, not to stay."

"Quite some adventure, eh?"

The lad shot a bright glance toward him.

"Yes."

"Well, well! Count yourself lucky, youngster, that you've had a good home and a good mother up to now; and bless your stars, too, that since you are going to start branching out you're coming to a place like Surfside rather'n somewhere else."

His voice was gentle and his misty eyes mistier than ever.

Striding ahead he crossed the lawn, unlocked a low building, and mounting the stairs, stopped before a door in the hall above. With a turn of the key it swung open, disclosing a small sheathed room containing a white iron bed, bureau, table, chairs, and bookshelves.

"Think this will suit your Highness?" grinned he.

"It's—it's corking!" stammered Walter, almost too delighted to reply.

"'Tain't bad," admitted Jerry, strolling over to one of the windows that faced the sea and looking out. "Mr. Crowninshield makes it a rule never to stow away other folks where he wouldn't be stowed himself. It isn't a bad principle, either. You'll have a couple of the chauffeurs for company." With his thumb he motioned to other rooms flanking the narrow hall. "They may josh you some at first. That's part of starting out in the world. Keep a civil tongue in your head and if you don't mind 'em they'll soon quit. If they don't it's up to you to find the way to get on with 'em. Half of life is learning to shy round the corners of the folks about you. And old Tim, who used to be gardener for Mr. Crowninshield's father and has been in the family 'most half a century, bides here, too. A rare soul, Tim. You'll like him. Everybody does. Simple as a child, he is, and so gentle that it well-nigh breaks his heart to kill a potato bug. You can count on Tim standing your friend no matter what the rest may do, so cheer up."

"And the dogs?"

"Oh, the kennels, you mean? They're close by where you'll get the full benefit of the pups' barking in the early morning," said Jerry, with a twinkle. "'Twill give you a pleasant feeling to be certain your charges are alive. Most often, though, they do no yammering until about six, and goodness knows all Christians ought to be up at that hour. You'll find the dogs fitted out comfortable as the rest of us. They've a fine enclosure to stay in when they want to be out of doors; a big airy room if it's better to have 'em under cover; steam heat when it's cold; and blankets and brushes without end. Sometimes Lola, the pet of 'em all, sleeps up at the big house; but mostly she's here with the rest. There's too big a caravan of 'em to have the lot live with the family. Besides, the folks like to sleep late in the morning and not be disturbed by the noise of a pack of puppies. Then there's guests here off and on. So take it all in all, the dogs are best by themselves."

"But I don't know anything about taking care of dogs," faltered Walter.

"I thought you'd had a dog yourself."

"So I had once. But he wasn't like any of these. He was just a dog. All you had to do was to chuck him a bone."

"Well, you'll have a darn sight more to do for these critters than that," announced Jerry.

"But how'll I know——" began the boy, alarmed by the prospect before him.

"Oh, you'll get your instructions from the Madam, most likely—get 'em all written down in black and white along with the history of every dog. She'll tell you just what every one of 'em is to eat, and how much; and where they're all to sleep. And if she don't Miss Nancy or Mr. Dick will. You'll get yards and yards of directions before you're through," chuckled Jerry. "You want to listen well to every word you hear too, son, for these dogs ain't like your Towser—or whatever his name was; a crumb of food too much might kill 'em. Or a blast of air."

"Scott!"

"Oh, there's no use getting panicky at the outset," declared Jerry comfortably. "Follow orders and use your brains; and remember that if you get addled you can always consult Tim. Tim has a world of common sense and a heap of knowledge of odd sorts. And more than that, he's never swept off his feet by the cost of things. Having been brought up in the company of Rolls-Royce cars, and diamond rings, and thousand-dollar dogs they don't move him an inch. He just treats 'em same's he would anything else and often it's the best plan. Instead of losing his head, and standing wringing his hands 'cause the prize roses have got bugs on 'em he sets to work and kills the bugs; sprays the plants same's he would ordinary bushes, and they go to growing again like any other civilized flowers. An orchid ain't no more to him than a buttercup. He's too used to 'em. He's used to dogs as well, and with the shifting fashions he's seen during his fifty years with the family he's had experience with most every kind of dog that ever was. For there's fashions in dogs, you know, as well as in coats and hats. So turn to Tim when you're in a tight place. He'll help you, never fear."

"I hope he will," sighed His Highness ruefully. "I shall need him."

"Nonsense! Why, Mr. Dick has often cared for the pups when there was no one else; and certainly you ought to have as many brains as he."

"Tell me about him."

"Richard? You've seen him round town lots of times—you must have. At the village and other places."

"Oh, of course I've seen him," agreed Walter quickly. "In the summer he drives past our house almost every day in his car. But I don't know him any."

"You will now," asserted Jerry. "He's a great chap, Mr. Dick is! About your age, too, I guess. Quite a mechanic and always tinkering with tools and machinery. If there's anything wrong with the motor boat he can usually fix her up all right. As for mending a car, he beats all the chauffeurs out. They know it and have to say so. Likely you've seen him fluking through the main street in his racer. She's a trim little thing and could go like the wind if his Pa hadn't forbidden letting out the engine. I reckon Mr. Crowninshield is afraid he'll either kill himself or somebody else, and I will own the thing ain't no proper toy for a lad his age. Still, city folks ain't content with what would please you or me. They must have the biggest, the fastest, the most expensive article there is or 'tain't good for nothin'. The mere knowin' it's the biggest, fastest, and cost the most seems to make 'em happy somehow. Funny, ain't it?"

His Highness did not reply. He was thinking.

"And Miss Nancy?" interrogated he presently.

"Ha! There's a girl for you!" ejaculated Jerry with enthusiasm. "She'll be either seventeen or eighteen come June. Swims like a fish. In fact, I ain't sure she couldn't outdistance some of 'em. And such an oar as she pulls! It's strong and steady as any man's. Besides that, she can beat the crowd at tennis, golf, and those other fool games such folks play. Has a runabout of her own, too, and drives it neat as a pin."

"She's better at sports than Mr. Dick, then."

"Oh, she can wipe the ground up with him," sniffed Jerry. "She can swim overhand to the raft and get back almost before her brother has started. By Guy! I never saw a woman swim as she does! Dick gets kinder peeved with her sometimes when she jollies him. But let her car play a prank and he has her, for she's no more idea what to do with an engine than the man in the moon. She treats brother Richard with proper respect then, I can tell you."

Walter smiled.

"And Mrs. Crowninshield?"

"She? She's all right! You'll like her and she'll like you—that is, if you get on with the pups. Dogs are her hobby. What she don't know about raisin' 'em ain't worth knowin'. But I just warn you not to think that because she's so pleasant she's easy goin', 'cause she ain't. Slip up on your job and she'll be down on you like a thousand of brick. She's a fair-weather sailin' craft—that's what she is; floats along nice as anything until something goes wrong and then—my soul—but she kicks up a sea. Yet with all that you'll like her. We all do. Almost everybody on the place would get down and let her walk on 'em. She has a kind of way with her that makes you itch to please her. Tim would let her cut his head clean off if she wanted to and I ain't sure I wouldn't. Have a smart sore throat once and see the things she'll do for you. And she'll do 'em herself, too—not set other people on the job. I believe that woman has the biggest heart in the world."

"And—and—Mr. Crowninshield?" ventured Walter.

"The boss?" Jerry cleared his throat and for the first time hesitated. "You've got to understand the boss, my son," said he earnestly. "He ain't like other men. And in order that you may, I better give you a pointer or two for it will most probably save you trouble. The boss is something like a big dog that barks fit to murder you and don't mean a thing by it. You've seen the kind. To hear him go on when he's roused you'd believe he was going to have your blood. My, how he does orate!" Jerry smiled and shook his head indulgently. "I've seen the men stand up before him with their knees shaking until you'd expect 'em to give way every second. And the master would rage and rage because they'd done something he didn't want done. And then, like a hurricane that's blown itself out, he'll calm down and the next you know he's given you a smile that's made you forget all the rest of it. That's him all over. Learn not to be afraid of him, that's the only thing to do. He wouldn't hurt a fly really. He just gets to blusterin' and tearin' round from force of habit. It don't mean nothin'—not a thing in the world. And with all his money he ain't a mite cocky. To see him you'd scarce dream he had a copper in his pocket. Yet he could paper the house with thousand-dollar bills was he so minded. There's no end to his money, seems to me. Just the same, you don't want to go wastin' it for him on that account. Remember you ain't got the right to, not havin' earned it. If he chooses to splash it round that's his hunt. He made it. But it ain't yours or mine to slosh away. Jot that down in your log. It may help you later."

Jerry paused.

"You deal square and honorable with the boss, standing up to what you've done like you was a trooper at your gun, and he'll deal square and honorable with you. But go to hoodwinking and imposing on him and instead of a lamb you'll find you've got a rattlesnake at your heels. Now you have an idea, I guess, what you're going to be up against here," concluded the caretaker, taking out his pipe and cramming it with tobacco. "If there's anything else you want to know now's your chance, for after to-day I am never going to open my lips again about any of the

Crowninshield family. You'll be one of the employees and your job will be to hold your tongue on them and their affairs, and be loyal to 'em. Their bread will be feeding you and 'twill be only decent. After you once have got your place the keeping of it will rest with you. That's fair, ain't it?"

Walter nodded.

Yet he turned slowly toward home, depressed by a throng of misgivings. Suppose he was not able to hold the job at Surfside once it was his? What then?

CHAPTER III

WHAT WORRIED MRS, KING

By the middle of May Lovell's Harbor had fully awakened from its winter's sleep. Freshly painted dories were slipped into the water; newly rigged yawls and knockabouts were anchored in the bay; the float was equipped with renovated bumpers, and a general air of anticipation pervaded the community.

Yes, hot weather was really on the way. Already the summer cottages were being opened, aired, and put in order, and even some of the houses had gayly figured hangings at the windows and a film of smoke could be seen issuing from the chimneys.

At Surfside workmen bustled about, hurrying across the lawn with boards, paint pots, and hammers. Tim Cavenough and his little host of helpers scurried to uncover the flower beds, and from morning to night trudged back and forth from the greenhouses bearing shallow boxes of seedlings which they transplanted to the gardens. Shutters were removed and stored away, piazza chairs brought out, awnings put up, and lawns and tennis courts rolled and cut.

As far as one could see a spangled expanse of ocean dazzled the eye and the tiny salt creeks that meandered across the meadows were like winding ribbons of blue. Certainly it was no weather to be shut up in school and boys and girls went hither with reluctant feet, checking off the days on their fingers and even counting the hours that must drag by before they would be free to roam at will amid this panorama of beauty.

To Walter King it seemed as if the closing period of his captivity would never be at an end. He studied rebelliously, and with only a half—nay, rather a quarter—of his mind on his lessons. All his thought was centered around Surfside and the novel experiences that beckoned him there. So impatient was he to begin his new duties that he found it impossible to settle down to anything.

"You'll be failing in your last examinations, Walter, if you don't watch what you're doing," cautioned his mother. "And should you do that, little profit would it be that you are hired out to Mr. Crowninshield for the summer. In the fall you'd have to stay behind your class, and think of the disgrace of that! Why, I'd be ready to hide my head with shame! Money or no money, you must buck up and put the Crowninshields and their doings out of your head. To lose a year now would mean just that much longer before you could graduate and take a regular job. I almost wish Jerry Thomas had never asked you to come up there, I do indeed."

"Oh, don't go getting all fussed up, Ma," returned His Highness, irritated because he recognized the truth of his mother's words. "I'm going to buckle down until the term is over, honest I am. It is hard, though, with the weather so fine. It seems as if I must be out. It's like being on a leash."

"You're thinking of those dogs again!"

The lad flushed sheepishly.

"No, I wasn't."

"But you were—whether you realized it or not. It is all you talk of nowadays—*dogs*! What it will be after they get here and you're up at Surfside living with them I don't know. Whatever else you do, though, you must not fail in your lessons and at the last moment spoil your whole year's record. School is your first duty now and you have no moral right to put anything else in its place."

"I know it, Ma," Walter agreed.

"Of course you know it," was the tart response. "Just see that you do not forget it, that's all."

With this final admonition Mrs. King whisked about and taking up her cake of Sapolio and pail of steaming water ascended the stairs. Like the rest of Lovell's Harbor she was busy as a bee in clovertime. She had rented all her rooms and had so many things to do in preparation for her expected guests that she had not a second to waste.

After she had gone Walter loitered in the kitchen, whistling absently and at the same time winding a piece of string aimlessly over his fingers. His mother's words had stirred a vague, uncomfortable possibility in his mind. What if he were to fail in those final exams? It would be terrible. Such a disaster did not seem real. It couldn't happen—actually happen—to him. It would be too awful. Nevertheless, try as he would to banish them, visions of Surfside with its myriad fascinations would dance in his head.

He had never been away from home for more than a night before and to take up residence elsewhere for an entire season was in itself a novelty. Then there were the tennis courts, the golf links, the automobiles, motor boats, and the yacht! Why, it would be like fairyland! The next instant, however, his spirits drooped. It was absurd to imagine for a moment that he was to have any part in those magic amusements. He was not going to Surfside for recreation but for work. Notwithstanding that fact, though, it was beyond his power to forget that all these many activities would be going on about him and there was the chance, the bare chance, that an occasion might arise when he would be invited to participate in some of them.

Fancy spinning over the sandy roads of the Cape in that wonderful racing car! Or sailing the blue waters of the harbor in one of those snowy motor boats! As for the yacht, with its trimmings of glistening brass and spotless decks, had he not dreamed of going aboard it ever since the day it had first steamed into the bay two summers ago? People said there was every imaginable contrivance aboard: ice-making machines, electric lights, and electric piano, goodness only knew what! Simply to see such things would be wonderful. And if it ever should come about (of course it never would and it was absurd to picture it—ridiculous) but if it ever *did* that he should go sailing out of the bay on that mystic craft what a miracle that would be!

With such visions floating through his mind what marvel that it was well-nigh out of the question for Walter King to focus his attention on algebra, Latin, history, and physics. X + Y seemed of very little consequence, and as for the Punic Wars they were so far away as to be hazy beyond any reality at all.

Possibly, although she was quite unconscious of it, some of the fault was his mother's for she kept the topic of his departure to the Crowninshields' ever before him.

"I have your new shirts almost finished, son," she would assert with satisfaction, "and they're as neat and well made as any New York tailor could make them, if I do say it; and you've three pairs of khaki trousers besides your old woolen ones and corduroys. With your Sunday suit of blue serge and those fresh ties and cap you'll have nothing to be ashamed of. Then you've those denim overalls, and your slicker, and Bob's outgrown pea-coat. I can't see but what you have everything you can possibly need. Do be watchful of your shoes and use them carefully, won't you, for they cost a mint of money? And remember whenever you can to work in your old duds and save your others. You can just as well as not if you only think of it. Your washing you'll bring home and don't forget that I want you to keep neat and clean. Rich folks notice those things a lot. So scrub your hands and neck and clean your nails, even if I'm not there to tell you to. Just because you are going to traipse round with the dogs is no excuse for looking like 'em," concluded she.

"I'll remember, Ma," returned His Highness patiently.

"And if you eat with the chauffeurs and a pack of men, don't go stuffing yourself with food until you're sick. There's a time to stop, you know. Don't wait until you've got past it and are so crammed that you can't swallow another mouthful."

"I won't, Ma," was the meek response.

"Brush your teeth faithfully, too. I've spent too much money on them to have them go to waste now."

"Yes," came wearily from Walter.

"Of course there's no call for me to talk to a person your age about smoking," continued his mother. "When you've got your full growth and can earn money enough to pay for such foolishness you've a right to indulge in it if you see fit; but until then don't start a habit that will do you no good and may make a pigmy of you for life."

"I promise you right now, Ma, that I——"

"No, don't promise. A promise is a sacred thing and one that it is a sacrilege to break. Never make a promise lightly. But just remember, laddie, that I'd far rather you didn't smoke for a few years yet. But should you feel you must why come and tell me, that's all."

"I will, Ma," answered the boy soberly. Somehow going away from home suddenly seemed a very solemn business.

"I guess that's the end of my cautions," smiled Mrs. King, "the end, except to say that I hope you won't like Surfside so well that you'll forget to come home now and then and tell me how you are making out. Of course I'll have my boarders and work same's you; still, there'll be times when we won't be busy and can see each other," her voice trembled a little. "Nobody will be more anxious to hear of your doings than I—remember that. I shall miss you, sonny. It's the first time you've been away from me and I can't but feel it's a sort of milestone. You'll be getting grown up and leaving home for good now before I know it, same as Bob has."

Her eyes glistened and for an instant she turned her head aside.

"Oh, I shan't be branching out to make my fortune yet, Mother," protested Walter gayly. "I don't know enough. I'm not clever like Bob—you said so yourself only the other day."

"You're clever as is good for you," was the ambiguous retort. "I'm glad you're no different."

"Think of the money I'd be handing in if I could only earn as much as Bob."

"The money? Aye, there's no denying it would be a help. However, with what you and Bob and I are going to earn this summer we should make out very well, even if your Uncle Mark Miller has left us in the lurch and your Uncle Henry King's investments have gone bad on us. I'll be turning a tidy penny with my boarders, thanks to you. And for a lad your age ten dollars a week is not to be sneezed at. Why, we'll have quite a little fortune between us!"

He saw her face brighten.

"Now if Bob could only be near at hand like you I believe I should be entirely happy," she sighed. "I hate to think of him way out there on that spit of sand with the sea booming all around him and nothing for company but the other fellow, who's asleep whenever he's awake, and that clicking wireless instrument. Imagine the loneliness of it! The solitude would drive me crazy inside a week—I know it would."

"Bob doesn't mind."

"He's not the lad to say so if he did," replied the mother grimly. "Nobody'd be any the wiser for what Bob thinks. Often at night I fall to wondering what he'd do was he to be taken sick."

"Oh, he'd be all right, Mother," answered His Highness cheerfully. "O'Connel is there, you know."

"And what kind of a nurse would he be, do you think, with his ear to that switchboard from daylight until dark?"

"Not quite that. Mother."

"Well, almost that, anyhow. It is all well enough for you to say so jauntily that Bob doesn't mind being off there with the wind howling round him and nothing to do but listen to it."

"Nothing to do!" repeated Walter. "Why, Ma, he's busy all the time."

"Tinkering with those wires, you mean?" was the indignant question. "Yes, I grant he has plenty of that, especially in bad weather. But I mean pleasures——"

"Moving pictures, church sociables, strawberry festivals," interrupted the lad mischievously.

"Yes, I do," maintained Mrs. King stoutly. "Folks must have something to brighten up their lives. Bob doesn't have a thing."

"He often has days that are lively enough, according to his stories."

"When there's wrecks, you mean?" She shook her head

gravely. "It isn't those that I'm talking about. It's sitting day after day and listening to the meaningless taps and buzzings that come whining through that instrument."

"They're not meaningless to him."

"No-o, I suppose not," sighed the woman. For a moment she paused only to resume her complaints. "Then there's the responsibility of it. I never did like to think of that. Should he tap once too much or too little when sending one of those dot and dash messages, think what it might mean! And suppose he heard a dot too much and didn't get the thing the other fellow was trying to tell him straight?"

"But he has been trained so he does not make mistakes."

"All human clay makes mistakes," was the tragic answer, "although I will say Bob makes fewer than most. And then the thunder storms—I'm always worried about those."

"Yes, I'll confess there is some danger from lightning," owned Walter unwillingly. "And of course there is danger from the current at all times if one is not careful. Even then accidents sometimes happen. However, Bob explained once that accidental shocks seldom result fatally unless the person is left too long without help. The man in charge of the radio outfit would almost never get the full force of the current, because part of it would be carried off through the wires and ground. Such accidents are mainly due to the temporary and faulty contact of the conductors."

"I can't help what they're due to," sniffed Mrs. King. "The point is that Bob might get knocked out and die."

"Nonsense, Mother. You would not worry if you understood more about it. Besides, should a man get a shock, if you go promptly to work over him and keep at it long enough, you can almost always bring him back to consciousness. They do just about the same things to restore him that they do for a person that's been drowned. The aim is to make him breathe. If you can get him to, he will probably live. Of course, though, you have to break the circuit first."

"The circuit?"

"Stop the current that is going through his body," explained Walter.

"But how can you?"

"Bob told me how. He saw a chap knocked out once and helped fix him up. You had to be awfully careful about moving him away from the apparatus, Bob said, or you might get a shock yourself. They took a dry stick because it was a nonconductor of electricity, you know, and rolled the man over to one side, so he was out of reach of the wires. Had you covered your hands with dry cloth you could have moved him, too; rubber gloves are best but Bob did not happen to have any handy at the minute. So they poked the fellow out of the way with the stick, turned him over on his back, loosened his collar and clothing, and went to work on him. You know how they always roll up a coat or something and stuff it under drowned persons' shoulders to throw their head backward? Well, they did that; and afterward they began to move his arms up and down to make him breathe. The idea is to depress and expand the chest. We learned it in our 'first aid' class. Of course there are lots of things you have to do besides, and if you can get a doctor he will know of others that are better still. But Bob said the chief point was not to get discouraged and give up. Sometimes people die just because the folks fussing over them do not keep at it long enough. They get tired and when they see no results they decide it is no use and stop trying. You ought to work an hour anyhow, repeating the exercises at the rate of sixteen times a minute, Bob said. Then, if the poor chap does not come to, you can at least feel you have done all you can."

"Ugh! It makes me shiver to think of it!"

"You didn't shiver when Minnie Carlton fell off the float and almost got drowned," remarked Walter significantly.

"I had too much to think of," was Mrs. King's laconic reply.

"It was the fussing you did over her that saved her life."

"They said so."

"You know it was."

"Mebbe it was," admitted his mother modestly. "But it wasn't any credit to me. I've always lived near the water and I feel at home with drowned people."

"These electric accidents are much the same—easier, if anything, because the lungs are not filled with water."

"I hadn't thought of that."

"This is just a straight case of making a man breathe. You did that for Minnie."

"I contrived to, yes."

"Well, this stunt is the same. Bob said if you once got that through your head and kept in mind what you were driving at instead of flying off the handle you would get on all right."

"Perhaps he's right. He generally is," sighed Mrs. King. "Still it is a worrisome business having him tinkering with those wires all the time. I am thankful you are not doing it. I'd rather you tended dogs."

"But you've forgotten what they're worth," put in His Highness.

"So I had. Oh, dear! I don't see but what I've got to worry about both of you."

"Pooh, Ma! Don't be foolish. Think of the money we'll have by fall, the three of us. Why, we'll be rich!"

"Not rich, with that last payment on the mortgage looming ahead."

"But it *is* the last—think of that! We won't ever have another to make."

A radiant smile flitted over Mrs. King's face but a moment later it was eclipsed by a cloud.

"There'll be other things to pay; there always are," fretted she.

"Oh, shucks, Ma! Why borrow trouble? It's always hanging round wanting to be borrowed. Why gratify it?"

"I know. It is a foolish habit, isn't it? Still, it was always my way to be prepared for the worst. I've done it all my life."

"Then why not whiffle round now and just for a change be prepared for the best?"

In spite of herself his mother laughed.

"I expect that if I was as young as you and as happy-go-lucky I'd never worry," she answered not unkindly. "But since I'm made with a worrying disposition and bound to worry anyhow, at least I've got something perfectly legitimate to worry about this summer, and you can't deny it. With one son liable to be electrocuted by wireless and the other likely to be run into jail for losing a million-dollar dog I shall have plenty to occupy my mind, not to mention all those boarders that are coming."

"Now, Ma, you know you are actually looking forward to the boarders," Walter declared. "Already you are simply itching to see them and find out what they are like."

"And if I am, what then?" admitted his mother flushing that she should have been read so accurately. "Seeing them isn't all there is to it by a good sight. There is feeding them, and to keep them filled up in this bracing climate is no small matter."

"Did you ever know any one to go hungry in this house?"

"Well, no; I can't say I ever did."

"Do you imagine boarders will eat more than Bob or I?"

"Mercy on us! I hope not."

"Well, you always gave us enough to eat. I guess if you contrived to do that you needn't worry about your boarders," chuckled His Highness.

CHAPTER IV

WALTER MAKES HIS BOW TO HIS EMPLOYER

The last day of June dawned dismal and foggy. A grim gray veil enshrouded Lovell's Harbor, rendering it cold and dreary. Had one been visiting it for the first time he would probably have turned his back on its forlornity and never have come again. The sea was wrapped in a mist so dense that its vast reach of waves was as complete a secret as if they had been actually curtained off from the land. On every leaf trembled beads of moisture and from the eaves of the sodden houses the water dripped with a melancholy trickle.

It was wretched weather for the Crowninshields to be coming to Surfside and yet that they were already on the way the jangling telephone attested.

"I wouldn't have had 'em put in an appearance a day like this for the world!" fretted Jerry Taylor, who for some unaccountable reason seemed to hold himself responsible for the general dampness and discomfort. "Fog ain't nothin' to us folks who are used to it. We've lived by the ocean long enough to love it no matter how it behaves. But for it to go actin' up this way for strangers is a pity. It gives 'em a bad impression same's a ill-behaved child does."

"But you can't help it," ventured Walter, who had just come into sight.

"N-o. Still, somehow, I'm always that anxious for the place to look it's prettiest that I feel to blame when it doesn't."

The boy nodded sympathetically. Deep down within him lay an inarticulate affection for the hamlet in which he had been born and the great throbbing sea that lapped its shores. He therefore understood Jerry's attitude and shared in it far more than he would, perhaps, have been willing to admit. Nevertheless he merely knocked the drops from his rubber hat, muttered that it was a rotten day, and loitered awkwardly about, wondering just what to do.

At last school was at an end. He had squeaked through the examinations with safety if not with glory, and having wheeled his small trunk up to Surfside on a wheelbarrow and deposited it in his room he speculated as to what to do next. There was plenty he might have done. There was no question about that. He might at the very moment have been unpacking his possessions, hanging his clothes in the closet, and stowing away his undergarments in the chest of drawers provided for the purpose. Moreover, there were books to tuck into place on his bookshelves and other minor duties relative to the settling of his new quarters.

Oh, there were a score of things he might have done. His Highness, however, was in much too agitated a frame of mind to turn his attention to such humdrum tasks. Furthermore, since he had pledged himself to bear a hand wherever it was needed, he felt he should be on the spot and within call. And if beneath this worthy motive lurked a certain desire to see whatever there was to be seen, who can say his curiosity was not pardonable? One does not set forth every day to make his fortune. The adventure was very alluring to him who had never tried it.

Possibly Jerry Taylor had enough of the boy in him to understand this. However that might be, he did not hurry the lad indoors to unpack even though he sensed full well that precious time was being wasted; instead, as he started across the lawn he called back over his shoulder:

"If you've nothing better to do, sonny, than to stand shivering in the barn, come along up to the house with me and help bring up some wood; I'm going to start fires burning in the rooms to cheer the folks up and dry 'em off when they get here. To my mind there ain't nothin' like an open fire to right you if you're out of sorts. And likely they will be out of sorts. Mr. Crowninshield will, that's sure. Now I myself don't mind a gray day off and on. It's sorter restful and calming. But these city people can't see it that way. My eye, no! They begin to groan so you can hear 'em a mile away the minute the sun is clouded over; and by the second day of a good northeaster they are done for. You'd think to listen to 'em that the end of the world had come. No motoring! No golf! No tennis! Why, they might as well be dead. They begin to wonder why they ever came here anyway and talk of nothing but how nice it is in New York. Why, you would split your sides laughing to hear Mr. Crowninshield moan for Wall Street and Fifth Avenue. Three days of fog is his limit. After that ropes couldn't tie him here. He tumbles his traps into a suitcase and off he goes to the city."

"Great Scott!" Walter ejaculated.

"Oh, 'tain't a bad thing to have him go, take it by and large. He ain't much addition here when he's fidgeting round, poking into everything and suggesting it better be done some other way. He's much better off somewhere else—he's happier and so are we. By and by he comes back again cheerful as if nothing had happened. Mebbe it's as well you should be told what's in store for you in foggy weather," concluded Jerry, with a touch of humor, "for you'll come in for your share together with the rest of us. Everybody gets it. Most likely you'll hear that an egg-beater is a much better thing to smooth down a dog's hair with than a brush; that all the world knows that and only an idiot uses anything else. Don't smile or venture a yip in reply. Just say you'll be glad to use the egg-beater if he prefers it. Remark that, in fact, you quite hanker to try the egg-beater. To agree with him always takes the wind out of his sails quicker'n anything else. He'll calm down soon as he sees you aren't ruffled and go off and hunt up somebody else to reform. And when the fog blows out to sea his temper will go with it and he will forget he ever suggested an egg-beater. Oh, we understand the boss. He's all right! If you only know how to take him you'll never have a mite of trouble with him."

By this time they had reached the house and having removed rubbers and dripping coats they entered the basement door and proceeded to the cellar. It was not the sort of cellar with which His Highness was familiar although his mother's cellar was clean, as cellars go. This one was immaculate. Indeed it seemed, on glancing about, that one might have done far worse than live in the Crowninshields' cellar. Every inch of the interior was light, dry, and spotless with whitewash, paint, and tiling. Even the coal that filled the bins had taken on a borrowed glory and shone as if polished.

"This is my kingdom!" announced Jerry proudly. "You could eat off the floor were you so minded."

"I should say you could!"

"When once you've set out it's no more work to keep things shipshape than to let 'em go helter-skelter. Now here's a basket. Load into it as many of those birch logs as you can carry and bring 'em upstairs. I've kindlings there already."

While Walter was obeying these instructions Jerry himself was piling up on his lank arm a pyramid of wood, and together the two ascended the stairway and tiptoed through the kitchen. As they went the boy caught a glimpse of gleaming porcelain walls; ebon-hued stoves resplendent with nickel trimmings; a blue and white tiled floor; and smart little window hangings that matched it.

"They don't cook here!" he gasped.

"Everything in the house is electric," explained Jerry, as if he were conducting a sight-seeing party through the Louvre. "All the baking, washing, ironing, bread-making, and cleaning is done by electricity. There's even an electric sewing-machine to sew with, and an electric breeze to keep you cool while you're doing it. If I hadn't seen the thing with my own eyes I'd never have believed it."

He paused to watch the effect of his words.

"'Tain't much like the way you and me are used to," he grinned.

"No."

"I suppose in time you get so nothing knocks the breath out of you. I'm just coming to looking round here without feeling all of a flutter. The place did used to turn me endwise at first, it was so white and awesome. I actually hated to set foot within its walls. Seems 's if my fingers was always all thumbs every time I come inside the room. Still, I had to come in though; there were things I had to do here. So I schooled myself to forget the whiteness, and the blueness, and all the silvery glisten and call it just a kitchen. Besides, I found that grand as it is, it ain't a patch on some of the other things in the house. My eye! It's like the Arabian Nights!"

The Cape Codder stopped quite speechless from retailing these marvels.

"Yes," he went on presently, "they've got almost everything the electric market has to offer. Last year, though, Mr. Dick got a hankerin' for a wireless set. It appears that you can buy an outfit that will make you hear concerts, sermons, speeches, and about everything that's going on; at least that's what Mr. Crowninshield undertook to tell me, though whether he was fooling or not I couldn't quite make out. Still, it may be true. After what I've seen in this house I'm ready to believe about anything. Was he to say you could put your eye to a hole in the wall and see the Chinese eating rice in Hongkong it wouldn't astonish me."

Walter laughed.

"You *can* hear music and such things. My brother, who is a wireless operator, told me so. They broadcast all sorts of entertainments—songs, band-playing, sermons, and stories so that those who have amateur apparatus can listen in."

"Broadcast? Listen in?" repeated Jerry vaguely.

"Broadcasting means sending out stuff of a specified wave length from a central station so that amateurs with a range of from two hundred to three hundred meters can pick it up."

Jerry halted midway in the passage.

"Do you mean to say," inquired he, "that a person can sling a song off the top of a wire into the air and tell it to stop when it's gone two hundred meters?"

"Something like that," chuckled Walter, amused.

"I don't believe it!" declared Jerry bluntly.

"But it can be done; really it can."

"No doubt you think you are speaking the truth, youngster," returned the skeptic mildly. "Somebody's stuffed you, though. Such a thing couldn't be, any way in the world."

As if that were the end of the matter Jerry opened a door

confronting him and stepped into the great hall, the splendor of which instantly blotted every other thought from Walter King's mind.

Not only was the interior spacious and imposing but it was bewilderingly beautiful and contained marvel after marvel that the lad longed to examine. The large tiger-skin rugs that covered the floor piqued his interest, so did the chiming clock, and a fountain that welled up and splashed into a marble pool filled with goldfish. Why, he could have entertained himself for an hour with this latter wonder alone!

There was, however, no leisure for loitering for on hearing the cadence of the chimes Jerry ejaculated in consternation:

"Eleven o'clock already! Land alive! We'll have to get the fires blazing lively. Why, the folks may be here any minute now. Here, hand me one of those long sticks you've got, sonny; or rather—wait! You know how to lay a fire, don't you?"

"I reckon I've done such a thing once or twice in my lifetime," was the dry response.

"Then go ahead. You build this fire while I go upstairs and start the others," said Jerry. "After you've got this one going you can make one in the library, that red room through those curtains."

"All right."

"Step lively! Don't take all day about it."

With awkward gesture Jerry swooped up some of the logs with his long arm and disappeared into the hall above.

As for Walter, he had built too many fires in his mother's kitchen stove and started too many blazes of driftwood on the beach to be at a loss as to how to proceed. Almost in a twinkling scarlet flames were roaring up the wide-throated chimneys and he had placed fenders before them to keep in captivity any straying sparks. While he looked about for a spot in which to deposit the remaining birch sticks there was a sound of horns, a crunching of gravel, and Jerry's scurrying feet came pattering down the stairs.

"It's the folks!" he announced excitedly. "We warn't a minute too soon. Tuck those logs into the brass box; pick up your cap, laddie, and light out of here quick."

The order, alas, came too late. His Highness had only time enough to hurry the birch wood into the box and bang down the cover before flying footsteps filled the house, maids appeared from every door, and there was a blast of wind, a babel of voices, and the discomfited boy found himself face to face with his employers.

His first impression of Mr. Crowninshield, muffled to the chin in a heavy motor coat, was of a large, red-cheeked man who, although he moved with little apparent stir, nevertheless in an incredibly short interval had shaken hands with most of the servants, directed where each piece of luggage was to be put, commented on a new lock on the front door, and noticed that the clock was two minutes slow. His moving eye had also been caught by the roses on the table and he turned to ask from which garden they came.

"All this he did, Ma," explained Walter to his mother afterward, "before you could say Jack Robinson. And in between he was scolding all the time about the weather and saying how idiotic it was to leave a warm, comfortable city like New York and come to a damp hole like the Cape."

"Is this the best day you could manage to get together, Jerry?" growled he. "Pretty beastly, I call it."

"It certainly is wet, sir."

"Wet! I should say it was! It's infernally wet! How long is it going to keep up like this?"

"I can't say, sir."

"Well, you have the sun out to-morrow or I shall go straight back where I came from. Little old New York is good enough for me when the place looks like this."

At that instant he espied His Highness lurking near a distant window.

"Who are you, young man?" he called.

"Walter King, sir."

"Oh, the young chap who is going to look after the dogs?"

"Yes, sir."

"Humph! Like dogs?"

"I—yes, sir," answered the lad at a warning glance from Jerry. Ruthlessly the hawklike eyes devoured him.

"So you think you can take care of a lot of prize pups, do you?"

"I am going to try," was the modest reply.

"You can't stop with trying, my son. You've got to do it," announced the man sharply.

"I shall do my best."

"That is all I shall ask."

A sudden smile melted the stern countenance into geniality and the master held out a hand.

"So King is your name."

"Yes, sir."

"It is a royal one and gives you something to live up to."

As the boy did not know what to answer he was silent.

"And you like dogs?" said the inquisitor more kindly.

"I like all animals," returned Walter evasively, "and I am sure I shall like your dogs because you always like anything you take care of."

"So you do! I remember when I was about your age I tamed an old brown weasel. He was a wretch of a creature with scarcely a virtue—cruel, deceitful, cold-blooded; and yet I grew to love that brute as much as if he had had the gentleness of a dove. You know how it is."

Walter nodded. For the moment the two came together on a plane of real contact and sympathy, and the smile the elder gave him bound the lad to his new employer as no spoken words could possibly have done.

But a second later Mr. Crowninshield's mood had changed and he was storming at Mary, the waitress, and demanding whether she meant to freeze them all by leaving the outside door open. Walter could see the girl flush red and as he leaped forward to close the door she flashed him a grateful, tremulous smile. Then Mr. Crowninshield turned toward his wife.

"Mollie," he replied, "this is Walter King who is going to look after your dogs. Come and speak to him."

The mistress of the house came. She was wearing a long blue traveling coat and a jaunty little hat against which the gold of her hair was resplendent as sunshine. Tucked under her arm was a wee dog with soft brown fur and sharp little eyes. Mrs. Crowninshield was very pretty, especially when she spoke. As Walter looked into her face he found it so amazingly youthful that it was difficult for him to believe she was actually the mother of a grown son and daughter.

"So it is you who are to be master of the kennels?" smiled she, showing her even white teeth.

"Yes, Mrs. Crowninshield," faltered His Highness, a trifle overcome by this new title.

From head to foot her glance swept over him.

"Well," said she at length, "if you keep the puppies as tidy as you keep yourself I fancy we shall get on nicely together."

A flood of color mounted to the lad's forehead. He had not

anticipated such close inspection and instinctively he began to fumble with the corner of his sweater and look nervously down at his hands. They must be very dirty from making the fires. And he had been actually greeting Mr. and Mrs. Crowninshield with paws like those! The horror of it chilled his blood.

Apparently the woman, with swift intuition, read his thought for she dimpled at him in friendly fashion.

"Do not worry about your hands, my boy," said she. "You have been doing useful things to soil them, things to bid us welcome and make us more comfortable. I can see you started out clean. I have a boy of my own, you know. Richard," she went on, turning to a tall youth who was bending over the luggage, "this is Walter King who is coming to look after the kennels. He must be about your age."

The boys stared at each other awkwardly.

"I am fifteen," announced Walter for the lack of something more brilliant to say.

"I beat you by a year," was the shy retort of the other boy. "I am sixteen."

Then Nancy interrupted them with her breezy comment.

"Fifteen, are you?" she put in. "My, I should not have thought it! You must be pretty crazy about dogs to give up all your summer vacation to them."

"My mother needs the money," was the simple answer.

"Oh!"

He saw her blush as if regretting her thoughtless remark.

"It is nice of you to help your mother," she observed quickly. "I am sure you will not find the place so bad. We shall try to make you happy."

With that she was gone but she left behind her a memory of sweetness and appealing kindliness.

"You might run out to the garage now, sonny," declared Jerry with a desire to help the lad make his escape. "They will be landing the pups there soon, and you may as well be on hand."

Only too glad to beat a retreat His Highness picked up his cap and slipping from the room raced across the lawn in the direction of his own quarters.

CHAPTER V

THE CONQUEST OF ACHILLES

Jerry's prediction proved to be quite true for as His Highness neared the garage a hum of activity pervaded it. Four mud-caked cars stood in the driveway and chauffeurs in their shirt sleeves hurried in and out the building, shouting to one another and carrying in their hands grimy rags and cans of oil. A short half hour had transformed the quiet spot to a beehive of noise and bustle. The rush seemed contagious for wherever one looked moving figures could be seen. Some crossed the lawn bearing belated satchels or traveling wraps which in the confusion had found their way into the wrong place; some strode toward the boathouse, some toward the garden, some to the stables. Men appeared to have risen through the earth so quickly had their numbers multiplied.

No longer was there the leisurely loitering and smoking that had marked the week before. A spirit of activity was infused into the air until even those who had no cause to hurry scrambled with the rest.

As Walter approached the garage he was waylaid by a young chauffeur with rosy cheeks and a crisp, pleasant voice:

"Say, youngster, don't you want to lend a hand with these cushions?" interrogated he, beaming ingratiatingly. "They have got to be beaten and brushed before they can go back in the car. Chuck them over on the floor for me, won't you?"

"Sure!" was the ready answer. "I'll beat them for you if you like."

"You're a good-natured little cuss," grinned the man. "I'm not asking you to do that, though."

"But I'd be glad to."

"Suit yourself. But in my opinion you are a fool to take on jobs you are not hired to do and get no money for."

"Oh, I don't care about the money."

"You don't, eh?" chimed in the derisive note of another chauffeur who had at the instant come out of the doorway. "Say, who are you, anyway? One of the Vanderbilts?"

"Quit heckling the young one, Peters," put in the chauffeur of the red cheeks. "He's a good sort, all right."

"Ha, ha, Wheeler! You think that because you've jollied him into doing your work for you, you old shirk."

"I didn't jolly him into anything. He offered."

"A likely story."

"But he did."

"Then you should have told him better," sniffed the other. "You know well enough it isn't etiquette round here to do a stroke of work for anybody else or accept a stroke. *Every man for himself* is the motto."

"But that's a rotten way!" Walter ejaculated impulsively. "I'd hate to live like that—never being willing to help anybody or ask them to help me."

The man called Peters gave him a contemptuous stare.

"You'll find there's no whining or asking help of other people here," announced he, with a sneer. "Those that are darn fools enough to get into holes get out of them as best they can. It's their hunt."

Spitting emphatically on the ground he proceeded to go into the garage with the tire he was carrying.

Walter took up a stick he saw lying near by.

"What are you going to do?" demanded the red-cheeked man, regarding him with unconcealed surprise.

"Beat the cushions."

"But—but—heavens, sonny! Didn't you hear what Peters said?"

"Of course I heard. I don't have to sign up to a creed like that, though, if I don't want to, do I?"

"We all do. We agree neither to borrow, lend, nor ask favors."

"I'm afraid I shan't make one of the gang then," observed Walter, with a smile so good-humored that the words could not offend.

"Then the more fool you, that is all I can say," laughed Wheeler. "By the end of a month you won't have so much as a collar button to your name. Everything you own will be gone, especially your tools. We're a lot of pirates. I give you fair warning."

"I'm not afraid you'll want much that I've got," grinned Walter.

The upraised stick descended in a series of rhythmic blows, sending into the air a cloud of dust.

"Where's the brush?" panted the boy, when he had beaten until his arm ached.

"Say, kid, I'm not going to have you breaking your back over my job," asserted Wheeler in a friendly tone.

"I'm not breaking my back."

"But what on earth are you doing it *for*?" questioned the man, his eyes narrowing with curiosity.

"I don't know myself," returned the lad shyly. "It was just the way I was brought up, I guess."

For an interval only the sweeping of the brush broke the stillness.

"I was brought up to be decent, too," observed Wheeler slowly, "but somehow since I've been knocking round I've got to be an awful brute. There isn't any very high standard among the crowd I mix in. Still, I'm afraid that isn't much of an excuse for shifting back into a savage." He paused thoughtfully, then added, "I'm much obliged to you, sonny, for your help, and just to show you I don't forget it, sometime when you are hard put hunt me up and ask me to give you a lift. I'm a human being though you may not think so."

With a little glow at his heart Walter moved away toward the kennels.

He had made a friend, and in this new environment where he was conscious of being very much of an outsider the consciousness brought him a sense of comradeship and happiness.

It was fortunate, however, that his altruism had detained him no longer for before he reached the spot where the dogs were to be quartered he heard a chorus of sharp yelps and saw what appeared to be a dozen dogs coming across the lawn accompanied by Mrs. Crowninshield and two of the stablemen. Some of the pack were being led, while others, wild with joy at finding themselves unconfined, leaped and capered wildly about their mistress. A great police dog, straining at the leash, gave Walter a thrill of mingled admiration and timidity. He was a huge creature with mottled coat and mighty jaws, and within his open mouth, from which lolled his red tongue, were cruel white teeth that could do unthinkable things. His wide brown eyes, his pointing tail, his upright ears moving with every sound, his alert poise all bespoke keenness and intelligence. A dog one would far rather have for an ally than an enemy, thought the boy.

Beside pranced two Airedales and a white Sealyham and to their babel of barking was added the shrill, sympathetic note of five or six Pekingese, one of which Mrs. Crowninshield carried under her arm.

"Hush, Achilles!" she cried. "Hush, all of you! Stop your racket this instant! They are excited at being together again," explained she to Walter who had approached. "The Belgian and Airedales have been boarded out during the winter and have not seen the others for months. So, you see, this is a sort of reunion for them and they have to bark to show their delight. Moreover, they have had a long trip and are tired and hungry. I am going to feed them now and this meal will last most of them until to-morrow at the same hour."

"Are they fed only once a day?" gasped Walter.

"That is all. You see you will not have many meals to prepare," laughed Mrs. Crowninshield. "Only the Peeks have breakfast, but only part of a square of puppy biscuit or some bread; so it is very simple. Dinner, however, is much more complicated and later I shall give you your directions as to just what every dog must have; to-night we are to treat the lot to some raw meat, toast, and spinach."

"You'll let me help you," pleaded Walter.

"Certainly. That is why I came out. I want you to feed the dogs and learn their names. In order to get on with them you must get acquainted with them and understand the peculiarities of each one. They are just persons, you know, and have their little whims and queernesses. But kindness will win them to you very quickly. It is far better than a whip. So is feeding. A dog usually obeys the person who feeds him. He is afraid not to."

As she spoke she entered the wired enclosure and putting the smaller dogs in half of it and shutting the wicket gate upon them she told the men to slip the leashes from the collars of the others. In a second the Belgian, Airedales, and the fluffy Sealyham were bounding about her. Then she beckoned to Walter.

"This is Achilles," went on she, with her hand on the head of the great monster. "He is as gentle and kind as a kitten, although he does look as if he could swallow us alive. Don't touch him but stand still and let him sniff you all over. It is his way of getting acquainted."

Obediently the boy remained motionless while the panting jaws and moist black nose of the dog came nearer. He could feel the creature's hot breath on his hands, face, and hair. Then over his clothing moved the quivering nostrils. At length the brown eyes met his and he whispered softly:

"Achilles!"

The dog wagged his tail.

"You have nothing to fear from him now," announced Mrs. Crowninshield. "The Airedales are Jack Horner and Boy Blue. And the Sealyham, Miss Nancy's dog, is called Rags."

Sensing that he was being talked about, the dog blinked with friendly eyes at Walter through its mop of coarse white hair.

"In the other pen," continued Mrs. Crowninshield, "are the Pekingese pups and I shall expect you to take the best of care of them. They are sensitive little creatures and very valuable. I myself, however, care very little for the money value of a dog. It is the lovable traits it has that interest me. I should adore wee Lola, here, if she were not worth a cent. But Mr. Crowninshield likes to own blue ribbon dogs and enter them at the shows and therefore I will caution you that Lola, Mimi, and Fifi," as she spoke she pointed out the dogs in question, "cost quite a fortune and their loss or illness would be a great calamity. So you must follow the directions concerning them most carefully. And should any question arise about them come at once to me."

As she spoke she occasionally glanced at the boy beside her with a quick, bright smile.

"I shall have the menu for each dog sent you every day—at least for the present—together with directions as to how to prepare the meal as it should be prepared. The meat for the small dogs must be put through a meat chopper and no gristle allowed to get into it; the larger dogs can have bigger pieces, and Achilles a bone. You will find in the room inside an ice chest in which to keep such foods as spoil. There are also glassed-in shelves where tins of various kinds of dog bread and puppy biscuit will be stored that they may be out of the dampness. You are not to trouble the servants at the big house for anything. They do not like to be interfered with. All your supplies will be here, and you can warm whatever it is necessary to heat on your small electric stove. Be sure to scald out the dishes after they have been used; and also never forget to keep the bowls filled with plenty of fresh water."

"I will, ma'am."

"I am sure you will," returned Mrs. Crowninshield kindly. "And do not worry if it takes a little time to win all the dogs over to your authority. Dogs are like children when they change masters. They will try to play it on you at first. Just be firm with them and soon you will have them tagging at your heels, docile as lambs."

The task of preparing the food was soon completed and the mistress looked on and encouraged while Walter doled it out to the famished animals.

How daintily the wee dogs coquetted with what was given them! And how greedily the larger ones gobbled down their allowance and lapped the plate for more! Achilles, crouched on the lawn with his bone, crunched it with terrifying zeal, cracking the big joint between his jaws as if it were made of paper. His dinner devoured he ambled over toward Walter, once more sniffed his shoes and clothing, at last nestled his moist nose against the boy's hand.

"I think you have won Achilles to your colors already," said Mrs. Crowninshield.

"He does seem friendly," returned His Highness, more pleased by the dog's good will than he would have been willing to own.

"Achilles can be very friendly when he chooses," retorted his owner. "He can also be quite the reverse. You should see him sometime when he is on the scent of a foe. Last summer when a man broke into the boathouse it transformed Achilles into a lion. I was certain he would kill the fellow; as it was he mauled him badly before we could coax him off. The thief almost died of fright and I do not wonder. He did not need any further punishment."

She unfastened the gate to go back to the house.

Immediately there was a rush.

"No, you can't come, not one of you," declared she, addressing the yelping pack through the netting. "I have far too much to do to be bothered with any of you. Be good and take a nap. You're tired enough to rest."

Still the animals barked, rebellious at their captivity.

"When I am out of sight you can let Achilles out," called she, as she moved away. "He can be trusted to roam the place and always does when we're here. The Airedales and the Sealyham can also run about alone as soon as they get used to obeying you. But the little dogs must never be let off the leash unless they are watched every instant, for something might happen to them."

"I'll be careful."

"That's right; do."

The woman gave him a pleasant nod of farewell and walked with springing step back in the direction of the house. As she went Walter saw her halt and speak to old Tim, who was at work in the rose garden, and beheld the gardener leap proudly forward to cut for her a blossom she had evidently admired.

It was even as Jerry had said. She was the idol of Surfside.

After she had disappeared he opened the wicket and stepped out, letting Achilles follow him.

Instantly the great creature put his nose to the ground and with a joyous bark he was gone in search of his mistress.

It was now or never with the new master of the hounds.

The lad whistled but the dog did not turn. Again he gave a quick call. This time the rushing beast paused, looked round, and then slackening his pace, continued to jog along on his way.

Helplessly the boy saw him go farther and farther out of reach.

He must compel obedience somehow.

"Achilles!" shouted he sternly. "Achilles! Back, sir!"

Although he uttered the words he had not the slightest faith they would have any effect and was amazed to see the dog waver in his tracks.

"Achilles, come here!" repeated he sharply.

With reluctance the dog turned and looked at him.

"Here, sir!" called Walter, with coaxing cadence.

The dog continued to regard him intently but he did not move. Then suddenly there was a rush and with panting jaws widespread the Belgian came bounding toward him. It was not until he was close at hand that he abated his speed. Then he came to the side of his new master and gently laid his cold nose on his sleeve.

Walter patted the great head affectionately.

The battle was won. He had conquered Achilles.

CHAPTER VI

HIS HIGHNESS IN A NEW ROLE

Before a week had passed the strangeness of living at Surfside had to a certain extent abated and Walter found himself not only content in his new position but enjoying it. He rose early, feeding the dogs, exercising them, and making fresh their quarters before he breakfasted himself. Afterward, despite the score of odd duties with which the morning was filled, he contrived to do many little kindnesses for Jerry, Tim, Wheeler, and the other men. He was always willing to do a favor and amid an atmosphere where generosity was rare the virtue of aiding others rendered him immensely popular.

In the meantime he had made such headway in the affections of Achilles that the big Belgian not only tagged at his heels everywhere he went, but at night insisted upon extending his giant frame before the boy's doorsill from which vantage ground neither threats nor persuasions could stir him. In consequence the lonely hours the lad might have experienced were put to rout by the companionship of this silent comrade.

The Airedales, on the other hand, were less successfully won over to a new allegiance. Although Richard, who owned them, took not the smallest care of them and serenely passed them over to some one else to be ministered unto, nevertheless they apparently sensed the arrangement was one of convenience and returned scant gratitude for what was done for them. They were polite, tolerant, but never whole-heartedly cordial. Dick was their master and they would have no other.

Fortunately Miss Nancy's Sealyham, Rags, was more responsive; nevertheless, although she frolicked about Walter's feet and accepted food from his hand it was more because she loved to play and was hungry than because her affection for the boy went very deep.

As for the troupe of Pekingese, with aristocratic noses tilted high in air, they submitted to being washed, brushed, and fed by Walter much as they would have accepted the services of any other maid or valet. They seemed to be conscious of their pedigree and claim attention as their right. An occasional wag of the tail or the rare passage of a rough little tongue across one's hand was all the gratitude His Highness ever received from them.

With the Crowninshield family, however, the boy made better progress and as he and Dick became acquainted many a pleasant hour did they spend together. Not infrequently, when the eager yelps of the dogs heralded the fact that they were off for their afternoon run, the New York lad would join the party and while the animals raced this way and that the two boys would discuss boats, fishing, and kindred interests.

"Do you happen to know anything about wireless?" inquired Richard one day when, with Achilles prancing far ahead and Boy Blue, Jack Horner, and Rags dashing to keep up with him, the group strode along the beach.

"I ought to," was Walter's smiling response. "I've a brother who is an operator at the Seaver Bay station."

"No! Really?" The exclamations voiced both surprise and admiration. "How old is he?"

"Twenty-two or three."

THE TWO BOYS WOULD DISCUSS BOATS,
FISHING, AND KINDRED INTERESTS.

"Gee! And he can really send and receive messages?"

"He sure can."

"How did he learn?"

"Oh, he first got interested in wireless through the papers and picked up quite a lot of information that way. Later he and his chum Billy Hicks bought a manual and with the help of the physics teacher at the High School they rigged up a homemade receiving apparatus on Billy's grandfather's barn. For a while it wouldn't work for a cent, although they tinkered with it night and day. Then one evening they did something to it and caught their first message. You should have seen Bob! He was crazy and came rushing straight home to make Ma drop everything she was doing and go down to Hicks's. Now Mother was elbow-deep in bread and declared she couldn't spoil her biscuit for any wireless on earth. Besides, she had never had any faith in the thing. You see, Bob had teased her for wireless money and she had told him time and time again it was dollars thrown into a hole. My father used to joke her about not having a scientific mind and I guess she hasn't one. At any rate, whenever Bob would read her the wonderful things being done with wireless, all she would say was that it wasn't likely folks could send speeches and music loose through the air. Those who pretended to hear them were either fibbing or were genuinely mistaken. So when Bob did get a broadcast you can imagine how wild he was to convince her it wasn't all bluff."

"And did he?" asked Dick with interest.

"Well, after a fashion," replied Walter, smiling at some amusing memory.

"Like enough I shouldn't have known much about it, either, if Bob had not told me," continued Walter. "Bob, however, talked nothing else morning, noon, and night. Often I would drop asleep while he was chattering of induction coils, wave lengths, and antenna. It makes me yawn now to think of it. My goodness, weren't Ma and I sick to death of hearing nothing but radio! Bob would rush into the house at mealtime, swallow his food whole, and tear off to Hicks's with a piece of pie in his hand, leaving all the chores to me. I got pretty sore, I can tell you." He gave a short laugh.

"Between Mother begrudging the poor chap every cent he spent for batteries and wire, and me pitching into him for forgetting to chop the kindlings, I'm afraid his early wireless career wasn't a very pleasant one."

Once more the lad laughed, this time with comic ruefulness.

"Even when the apparatus actually did begin to work and Bob and Billy were able to get a concert or lecture now and then, Ma insisted they were bluffing her. She listened in but wasn't convinced, declaring they had fastened a victrola to the receivers and that such sounds never could come through the air. Finally they did succeed in getting her to half believe they were telling her the truth and were not just working her for money. But when they tried to explain the outfit to her in detail, she put her hands over her ears, protesting that they were wasting their breath to tell her of damped and undamped waves, detectors, and generators. With that they gave up further attempts to educate her."

Both boys chuckled.

"But she must be proud of your brother now," asserted Dick.

"Oh, she is—tremendously, although what she chiefly thinks about is the danger Bob is in of getting struck by lightning or electrocuted."

Achilles, who had been pursuing some sandpipers along the rim of the surf and sent them circling into the air, now raced back to his friends with a sharp bark of salutation and Dick bent to pat the shaggy head.

"So really," reflected he, "your brother taught himself wireless."

"Not wholly. He simply laid a foundation," the other boy explained. "He could never have taken a job on what he had picked up because, you see, he knew nothing of sending messages, was ignorant of all the rules an operator has to have at his tongue's end, and had no very thorough knowledge of electricity. It was not like a complete training, by any means. The war gave him that. When it broke out he enlisted in the navy, and because he was partially equipped in radio they sent him off posthaste to a wireless school. At the time he was crazy because his dream was to get across and be in the fighting. To sit at home studying was the last thing he wanted to do. Later, though, when he began to see what a big part wireless was playing in the scrimmage, he commenced to be more resigned to his lot. Besides he got his chance before long, for he worked into being a crackerjack at speed and passed his exams so well that he had no trouble in winning his first-class operator's certificate.

"There are grades of radio men, you know, just as there are grades of everything else. There are the sharks, or first-class chaps, who are able to pass every sort of test on the adjustment of apparatus and how to use it; who can both send and receive messages at the rate of at least twenty words a minute, and who can often go much faster; and who have all the rules governing the exchange of radio messages stowed away in their heads. They are the A1 men and every first-class ship is obliged by law to have aboard it two of them. Then there are the second-class certificate fellows who practically have as much radio but cannot hit such a gait, and can only manage to send between twelve and nineteen words a minute. They can go on first-class ships provided more skilled operators are aboard. Sometimes, even, they substitute for them under supervision. Their chief jobs, however, are on ships that use wireless only for their personal benefit; that is, to talk with their own crews. Often a fishing fleet, for instance, will carry a man of this class to communicate with its other vessels. They can talk, too, with shore stations when it is necessary. But the law does not allow them to take positions where there is a great rush of business and general responsibility. They must have the topnotchers for such work."

"I had no idea there were so many rules about radio," mused Dick.

"There are—strict ones, too," replied his companion. "Moreover, the government keeps tabs on all radio people to see they obey the rules. Every wireless man is examined, classified, and given a license just as an automobile driver is. He has to keep it handy, too, and be ready to trot it out on request. You can't get by with bluffing. If an operator is found to be unfamiliar with the rules, or is discovered breaking any of them, his certificate can be withdrawn. No chap wants to risk that, especially if he is trying to earn his living by wireless. And if a ship, and not its radio operator, is found to be breaking the rules, the coastal stations may be notified not to have anything to do with her. In other words she is boycotted and the land operators told neither to receive her messages nor answer them."

"That would be some boycott!"

"The shipboard radio stations, you see, come under the authority of the commanding officer of the ship. It has to be so, because in case of accident he would be the person responsible for sending out distress calls and answering them. The radio man couldn't just grab the power. There has to be one boss of every job."

"I can see that," nodded Dick. "But why such a network of other rules?"

"There have to be. It all has to be charted in black and white or there would be terrible mix-ups."

"And do foreign ships have to fall into line and do as our ships do when they come here?"

"They are expected to, Bob said," answered Walter. "In case they do not, however, they cannot be meddled with by underlings. Instead they are immediately reported to the government and the two countries involved settle their dispute by arbitration. It is too delicate a matter for others to butt in on, for some blunderer might offend another country and get us into war just through being stupid. Conversely, when our ships are in foreign waters they must keep the naval rules of the nation they are visiting."

"That's fair."

"It sure is," agreed Walter. "Besides that, all the shipboard radio stations have to carry with them their license to prove that they are authorized by their countries to operate a wireless outfit, and that they fulfil the requirements of the government whose flag they fly. Should any trouble arise when they are in a foreign port they can be asked to produce this license; and if the foreign authorities whom they are visiting have reason to suspect they are not meeting the standards the license demands they can complain to the government that is responsible for the ship."

"But suppose the government didn't know anything about such a ship?"

"Great Scott! But it does, man," ejaculated Walter. "There

are lists that contain not only the name and nationality of all ships but even the names and addresses of its radio operators. There is no getting by that."

"So the ships themselves are not allowed to take up their own quarrel if they are challenged?" commented Dick.

"No. They simply have to stay perfectly polite and keep their mouths shut, no matter how mad they are," grinned His Highness. "Otherwise there would be squabbles all the time, for there are always misunderstandings and grudges, and people who enjoy picking on one another. All the ships would be fighting and the countries that owned them, too, if everybody rolled up his sleeves and pitched into the other fellow when things went wrong. Governments are supposed to be more slow-moving, fair, and impartial. And anyhow, it is their job to look out for their own citizens and see they are squarely treated. Bob says it is a more dignified way than for individuals to fight out their own quarrels. It certainly carries more weight. Nobody is going to bully a ship and make trouble for its crew if a big nation stands behind it. It serves as a check on the men, too, Bob told me, for when they are in other countries and have shore leave they have to remember that they must behave themselves and not disgrace their governments."

"You can't sail out of reach of Uncle Sam, eh? Apparently he knows in a general way just how you are conducting yourself all the time," smiled Dick.

"That's about it," acquiesced Walter.

Whistling to the dogs, they turned about.

"What a pile you know about all this," Dick presently observed.

"Shucks! No, I don't," blushed His Highness. "I am only repeating what Bob spieled off to me. He likes to talk when he's home and I like to listen. It's interesting—at least I think so. Besides, I'm proud of Bob knowing such a lot. I wish I did."

The lad dug his heel into the moist sand and watched the hole fill with water.

"Somehow I'm an awful boob at books," he suddenly confessed. "I hate so to study that Ma fairly has to haul me along by the hair or I'd never go to school. I barely skinned through this year. Up to the very last minute we all had cold chills for fear I wouldn't."

Dick shot the offender a sympathetic glance.

"I don't like reading about things myself so well as doing them," he confided. "I'm crazy about machinery. It's fun to tinker with it—take it to pieces and put it together again. I like nothing better than to overhaul an engine."

He held up two grease-stained hands.

"It horrifies my mother," he continued, "but my father doesn't seem to mind if I am all black with oil from my car or the motor boats. What I want now is a wireless outfit. I'm going to strike Dad one for my birthday. It comes the last of this month and he might as well give me that as anything else. Do you suppose if he got it we could rig it up together?"

Walter's eyes opened at the casualness of the observation.

In his family a birthday was an occasion for a chocolate cake, some neckties, and perhaps a pair of rubber boots or a similar useful gift. Or it sometimes brought with it a book and a box of candy. Never by any chance did its felicitations expand into a gift so colossal as a wireless apparatus. The breach between the two lads, which during the exchange of confidences had narrowed into nothingness, widened abruptly.

"A good set would be some present," he commented, thinking, perhaps, the other boy might be ignorant of its value.

"Oh, I guess it would not break Dad," smiled Dick serenely. "He gave me my car last year, and the year before—let me think—oh, the pups!" He pointed to the Airedales, a streak of buff against the green of the distant marsh. "Wireless couldn't cost much more."

"N—o, I don't believe it would," His Highness admitted slowly, the contrast in their financial standards seeping in on him.

"Oh, I imagine I could have a set all right if I said the word," continued Dick, with the indifference of one to whom such presents brought no agitation. "The question is, could we set it up if we had it?"

"I couldn't," came promptly from Walter. "I think, though, that if Bob was home on leave he might help us."

"Your brother? I had forgotten him. So he is at home sometimes?"

"Oh, yes. He gets off for a day now and then."

"It must be a whole lot of a bore to be tied down in a wireless station listening for messages all the time," observed Dick carelessly.

"Operators do not have to sit with their ears glued to the receivers every second, man," declared the village lad. "The men are relieved at regular hours. Besides, all stations both on shore and on shipboard are divided into classes and have their hours carefully mapped out for them. There are three different varieties of shipboard stations, for example. Some have constant service; that is, operators are always listening while the ship is underway. Then there is a second sort where the operator listens in only during specified hours when the office is open for business. A third class has no fixed hours at all, the radio man just listening the first ten minutes of each hour."

"So the men just suit themselves, eh?"

"Suit themselves! You bet they don't," laughed Walter. "The government defines their hours when their license is issued. The class they are put in decides it."

"That's news to me," said Dick. "And the shore stations?"

"The shore stations are a chapter in themselves," Walter replied. "There are several different kinds and each kind has its own rules."

"You don't propose to tell me about them, then," retorted the New Yorker mischievously.

"It's too long a yarn," answered the other. "Besides, I might not get it straight. Sometime, though, if you want me to, I'll pass on what I know. But to-day I guess we ought to be hiking back. It is close onto the time the pack is fed and I may have them yelping at my throat if I don't hurry."

Quickening their pace the boys whistled to the dogs who came dashing through the clumps of bayberry that dotted the field. They were panting with thirst and only too ready to turn homeward. Across the sandy hillocks, through pine-shaded stretches of woods, along the road walled in with June roses they raced and chased, stopping now and again to look back and make certain that their masters were following. When the spit of sand narrowed to a ribbon and the entrance to Surfside was reached they halted, lying down to cool off in the fresh sea breeze until they should be overtaken. At the gate Dick and Walter parted.

It was amusing to see the Airedales waver, then lured by hunger, desert their owner and pursue Walter and Achilles.

They came up with lolling tongues at the kennels just as His Highness was unlocking the door.

While he fumbled with the latch he noticed they sniffed excitedly about and that Achilles barked.

"You're starved, poor old chaps!" remarked he aloud. "Well, no matter. You shall have your dinner right off now."

Coaxing them in he banged the wicket behind him and passed through into the pen where the Pekingese, clamoring for their food, came yelping to meet him.

Instinctively he scanned the fluffy-coated group. Lola was not there.

The discovery, however, caused him no concern for often Mrs. Crowninshield carried the prize-winner up to the big house or took her for a ride in the car. Therefore, although her bright eyes were missing he did not worry, but fed the other dogs and gave them fresh water.

The task completed, he sauntered toward the garage.

How still it was everywhere. With the exception of Dick's racer every car was gone and all the chauffeurs with them. Even Jerry was nowhere about; and the gardeners were far down on the south slope where he could just detect the clip of their shears as they trimmed the privet hedge.

The grounds were as deserted as if the earth had swallowed up every inhabitant. Surfside, deprived of its accustomed hum and bustle, was actually lonely. With uncertain step the boy loitered in the sun, glancing at the expanse of sea and at a knockabout that heeled dangerously in the rising wind. Thinking he might find Jerry and thus banish solitude he meandered up the avenue toward the house.

Jerry, however, was nowhere to be seen but the silence was broken by the siren horns of approaching motors and the Crowninshield cars came rolling in through the broad entrance.

Since he chanced to be on the spot he may as well go up to the veranda, meet the family, and bring Lola back with him to be fed and tucked up for the night.

Accordingly he hurried along and was at the steps almost as soon as the automobiles came to a stop.

Together with a company of laughing guests, Nancy and Mr. and Mrs. Crowninshield alighted.

"Such a beautiful ride as we've had, Dick!" called Mrs. Crowninshield to her son. "We've been over to Harwich and picked up the Davenports, you see, and brought them home for the evening. I think, Mrs. Davenport, you remember my son, Richard. Nancy, take Janet and Marie in with you so they can leave their wraps. You young people will have just about time for a set of tennis before dinner."

The cars had shot away and she was about to go indoors when the mistress of the house espied Walter.

"Did you wish to see me?" she called.

"I thought I'd take Lola down to the kennels."

"Lola! Is she here?"

"I thought you had her."

"No, indeed."

"But she must be here at the house."

"No, she isn't. I never leave her with the maids. She is at the kennels."

"I've just come from there."

"And she wasn't there?"

"No, ma'am."

"Are you sure?"

"Positive!"

"But my dear boy, didn't you leave her there?"

"Yes. But I thought you took her when you went to drive. You have a key."

"I didn't."

"And you did not give the key to any of the maids?"

"Of course not."

"Well, she isn't there," announced Walter, a tremor of trepidation passing over him.

"Nonsense! She must be. Where else could she be?"

"I don't know."

"Oh, you haven't half looked," smiled Mrs. Crowninshield reassuringly. "Lola is such a tiny dog she often gets hidden away out of sight. I'll come and find her for you."

Excusing herself to her guests she followed Walter across the grass and in silence they unfastened the wire gate that led into the enclosure where the Pekingese were kept. But search as they would they failed to discover the missing dog. Lola was gone! *Gone!*

CHAPTER VII

THE PURSUIT OF LOLA

Yes, Lola was gone; there could be no question about that. Had not Walter scented trouble he would soon have been made aware of it by the excitement that prevailed in the Peeks' kennels. Every dog of the lot was barking furiously and with gleaming eyes and tail erect striving to communicate tidings of importance. Yet bark as they might, the message they sought to voice remained, alas, untold.

"If they could only speak we should soon know what has happened," bewailed the lad to Mrs. Crowninshield, as for the hundredth time they searched every nook and corner for a clue to the mystery.

"Yes, they know—poor little things," their mistress agreed. "They are trying their best to tell the story, too. I'd give worlds to know what it is."

"And I."

"You are certain you locked everything up when you took the other dogs out."

"Positive. Dick was with me and we both tried the gate before we started."

"Nothing seems to be disturbed."

"No. That is the strange part of it."

Mrs. Crowninshield stopped, hot and breathless from her search.

"I cannot believe but that the mite will turn up. Have you asked Jerry or Tim?"

"They were nowhere about when I got back," Walter replied. "The whole place was still as the grave. I was just going to hunt up Jerry when I saw the cars coming up the avenue."

"Well, I must not delay any longer now," announced Mrs. Crowninshield. "The Davenports will be wondering what has become of me and so will everybody else. Just find Jerry and Tim and quietly make sure they have not taken the dog. In the meantime I will inquire of the maids at the house. We will not, however, make too much talk about it, and send out an alarm until we are certain there is a real tragedy. If I can keep Mr. Crowninshield in ignorance of the matter until our guests have gone I shall be glad. He will be dreadfully upset for he took great pride in his possession of Lola and has declined numberless offers to sell her."

"I know it," groaned Walter. "If it were only one of the other dogs that was missing!"

"The fact that it isn't is what alarms me," returned the woman. "Lola is a quiet little thing and has been petted so much that it would not be like her to run away. Some of the other dogs might but she wouldn't. She is far too timid."

"How could she run away, even if she had a mind to, with the gate locked?"

"I know. That is another ominous fact." Mrs. Crowninshield shook her head. "I'm afraid———"

"What?"

"That she has been stolen."

"Stolen!" gasped Walter. "But how could she with—with everybody around?"

"But you yourself just said that nobody was around."

"Jove! That's true. Still somebody must have been here some time during the afternoon. It is not likely Jerry, Tim, and all the rest were out of hearing all the time I was gone."

"That is what we must find out."

"I'll go and hunt up Jerry now."

"Do. But work quietly; do not make a fuss. It will be time enough to get everybody up in arms when we have to. I dread to think what Mr. Crowninshield will say. He will be furious, simply furious."

With this dubious prediction his wife walked away.

She herself was upset. It was easy enough to see that. She strove, however, to be calm, clinging desperately to the hope that the dog might be discovered in the care of some of the men or maids. She idolized Lola and although she did not admit it, His Highness knew only too well that if it really proved that her pet was gone she, too, would be furious.

"A nice mess!" commented the lad to himself as he hurried across the lawn in search of Jerry. "A nice hole I am in the very first thing! Between them they will tear me to pieces. And Ma—Ma will say, '*I told you so!* That's all the sympathy I'll get from her. She'll have to know, of course, for Mr. Crowninshield will fire me bag and baggage. I must expect that. Jerry as good as told me so when I came. I sha'n't have a chance to defend myself. They will just believe I left the gate of the kennels unlocked when I went out and that Lola made off as fast as her four small feet could carry her. They will either think that, or they will think—" he stopped aghast at the possibility that had taken possession of his mind. "They couldn't think I left it open on purpose for some one to get in and *take* Lola! They couldn't think that! But suppose Mr. Crowninshield did decide I was an accomplice what proof have I but my word that I wasn't.

It does look bad—my being gone and taking Achilles and the other dogs with me. Still, I've done it every day since I've been here. And anyway, they would know I could not entice Jerry and Tim away even if I had wanted to."

The boy took courage.

"No, of course they couldn't think *I* had anything to do with Lola being gone," he murmured.

By this time he had overtaken Tim and his fellow workers who were still busy clipping the hedge.

"Tim!" he called.

There was no answer but the crisp snip, snip of the shears.

"Tim!"

"Did you call?"

"Yes. You haven't seen Lola, have you?"

"Lola? Indeed I haven't. What would she be doing round here, I'd like to know?"

His Highness struggled to smile.

"Oh, I just thought you might have seen her."

"She's not at the kennels?"

"No."

"Oh, then the mistress took her up to the house. She often does. She is clean daffy over that dog. Give yourself no concern, sonny; the pup is with the master and missis, being shown off to company, most likely."

"Probably she is. So you and the men have been here all the afternoon?"

"That we have. A hot job, the cutting of this hedge."

"It looks fine," declared Walter, turning away.

"It ought to," Tim growled. "Goodness knows it's trouble enough! A privet hedge is the devil to keep even."

Walter, however, did not wait to hear the virtues and vices

of privet hedges discussed. He was in too much of a hurry. Furthermore, he had secured the information which he had come to seek. Tim and his host knew nothing of the whereabouts of Lola. Nothing else mattered. In fact, bewildered, anxious, and excited, it seemed at the moment as if nothing else would ever matter again. He must find that dog—he *must*!

Nevertheless he remembered he must not appear agitated and therefore, instead of racing across the lawn and shouting for Jerry as would have been his inclination, he walked decorously along the path until he came to the boathouse from which door Jerry was at that instant issuing.

"You haven't seen Lola, have you, Jerry?" he asked as indifferently as he could.

"Lola? No. Why?"

"It—it is just her dinner time," stammered the lad, "and I wanted to find her."

"She'll be up at the house, most likely, if she isn't at the kennels," announced Jerry. "There's visitors and Lola will be on deck to see 'em. She's a vain little lady and likes to be shown off."

Walter greeted the remark with a sickly grin.

"What have you been doing?" inquired he idly.

"Me? Why, I was just starting to fix that hasp on the gate to the chicken coop when Minnie came running down from the house to say somebody wanted to speak to me on the telephone. It was a long-distance call and kept me there most half an hour; and what it was all about I don't know now. Some feller I never heard of kept talking and talking, and I couldn't make head nor tail out of anything he said. Finally I told him so and hung up the receiver. I can't imagine who he was. Nobody ever telephones me."

"So you didn't get the hasp fixed on the hen yard."

"I would have hadn't the cook held me up just as I was leaving and wanted I should put a new washer on the kitchen faucet. I saw it needed it the worst way. In fact, I had planned to do it before the folks came and it had slipped my mind. So I tinkered with that and got nothing else done. I'm just after mending a hinge on the boathouse door. A profitless afternoon, I call it."

"So you haven't been back to your diggings since noon."

"Not a once. Why? Did you want me?"

"N—o. Oh, no."

"That's lucky. Apparently everybody else did," concluded Jerry grimly.

So went Walter's quest! Nobody had seen Lola. Nobody knew anything about her. Question as he would, not the faintest trace of the missing dog could be obtained; and when the Davenports rolled down the drive the lad faced the awful moment when his secret must be divulged and the alarm sounded that Lola, the Crowninshields' most valued possession, was missing. Rapidly he turned the prospect of the coming storm over in his mind.

Since the dog had been left in his charge the only manly thing to do, he argued, was to go directly to Mr. Crowninshield and himself acquaint him with the direful tidings. It would be cowardly to shunt this wretched task off on somebody else. It was his duty and his alone. Nevertheless, as he stood for a moment summoning his courage, he would have given all he possessed to escape the interview that awaited him.

He would be scolded, blamed, discharged—that he knew— and he must bear bravely censure for something which he could not feel was his fault. Yet notwithstanding the fact that his conscience exonerated him it made the coming scene no less dreadful to anticipate.

If Bob were only at hand to offer him his advice and sympathy. Bob was such a bully comforter. He never jumped on a man when he was down. Besides, he had a level head and always knew exactly what to do in an emergency. The instant this awful talk with Mr. Crowninshield was over and he was actually "fired" he should call Bob on the telephone and tell him the whole story. He must tell somebody, and Bob would understand better than anyone else just how everything had happened.

In the meantime there was nothing to be gained by further delay.

Pulling himself together, His Highness (a very meek bit of royalty now) dragged himself up the flower-bordered path toward Surfside. As he went it seemed as if every pansy flanking the walk stared out at him and whispered, "Aha, young man! You're in for it now!"

Alas, he did not need to be told that! He knew it only too well. He cleared his throat, wondering how he should begin his confession.

"Mr. Crowninshield, I have some very sad news to impart to you—etc."; or "Mr. Crowninshield, I regret to say a very terrible thing has happened." Such an introduction was easily delivered. It was the next sentence that appalled him. He could not get it off his tongue. "*Lola has disappeared!*" He could see now the great man's face as it flushed with anger and surprise. What would *he* say—that was the question?

Probably his reply would be something like this.

"Young fellow, when I hired you, you undertook to look out for my dogs and see that nothing happened to them. I agreed to pay you good wages to perform that service and you, on your part, promised to do it satisfactorily. How have you kept that promise? You knew Lola's value and you should have looked out for her. It's up to you. You must either produce that dog or you must pay for her."

He had by this time reached the house and like a criminal who faces execution and mounts the scaffold steps he climbed the broad flight leading to the front door. Mr. Crowninshield was on the veranda, sitting quietly in a big wicker chair, looking out toward the sea. He was thinking so intently on some imagining of his own that he did not hear the lad's footfall and Walter was obliged to address him twice before he answered. Then he started suddenly, as if annoyed at being disturbed.

"Well?" interrogated he.

The fine introduction that His Highness had planned to utter, together with everything else he had arranged to say, fled from his memory and he stood speechless before his employer.

"You wish to see me?" Mr. Crowninshield repeated in a less sharp tone.

"I—yes, sir."

Nevertheless, despite the heavy pause the words the boy sought would not come. Instead a plaintive jumble of phrases tumbled incoherently forth, astounding the lad himself almost as much as they did the person to whom they were addressed:

"Oh, sir, I've lost your dog, Lola! I didn't mean to and I didn't really lose her. She was gone when I got back from my walk with Achilles and the others. I left her locked in all right—I know I did. Where she is or how she got out I've no idea. I'm terribly sorry. I can't possibly pay for her, and you'll just have to put me in prison. It's the only way, I guess. Don't blame my mother or Bob, please, or Jerry either, because I've turned out to be such a duffer. It isn't their fault. And perhaps I better go straight home. I suppose you won't want me round here any more."

A great gasp strangled any further utterance and only the lad's sobbing breath broke the stillness.

Nerved to receive a scourge of maledictions or a blow the

culprit waited. But nothing came—neither vindictives nor chastisement. He ventured to raise his head and confront his judge.

Mr. Crowninshield was sitting looking far out to sea exactly as before and Walter actually began to wonder whether he had been turned to stone or had been stricken with deafness.

"Mr. Crowninshield!" he at last ejaculated when the silence had become intolerable.

"Yes."

"Did you hear what I said?"

"Yes, sonny."

"Well—well—what are you going to do with me?"

"Nothing, my boy."

"*What?*"

"This job about Lola is nothing to do with you, my son. It has evidently been planned for a long time and carefully executed by professionals. Had you been on the spot they would have contrived to circumvent you just as they did Jerry. A gang have beaten us, that's all. But I will show them I am not to be beaten so easily. I'll have that dog back if it takes every dollar I have in the world. And I'll land those chaps behind the bars, every one of them, or my name isn't Crowninshield."

A tide of angry color surged over the face of the speaker and he rose abruptly, as if forgetting the lad's presence.

"Yes, sir!" he continued. "I'll round up those thieves. They needn't put me down for such an ass. Of course it's Daly and that New York bunch that set them on. They have always wanted Lola and been mad as hatters that I refused to sell her. Only the last time I saw Jake Daly he said, 'What I can't get by fair means I sometimes get by foul, Crowninshield, so you'd better look out for your precious dog.' I did not heed the threat at the time, attributing it to temper. But evidently he meant just what he said. He intended to have the dog, whether or no. But by thunder," Mr. Crowninshield brought down his fist on the piazza rail, "he won't win out in the deal! I'll jail him and all his tribe—see if I don't!"

Walter, watching, hardly knew whether to go or stay. The man's rage was terrible and he thanked his lucky stars that it was not directed toward himself.

"Is—is—there anything I can do, Mr. Crowninshield?" he at last managed to stammer after the master had ceased his pacing of the veranda and at length became conscious of his presence.

"Not a thing, little chap," returned his employer, flashing him one of his rare smiles. "You have been mighty white about this, though. I guess it took some nerve to come up here and tell me this, didn't it?"

"Yes, sir, it did."

"I wondered what you'd do."

"Wondered?"

"Yes. Mrs. Crowninshield told me about Lola the minute the Davenports went. I saw the affair had nothing to do with you. Nevertheless, I wasn't sorry to try you out and see how much of the man was in you. You're all right, boy. Cheer up! Nobody is going to pack you home to your mother, so don't worry. And far from blaming you, if I want help about finding Lola, I'll add you to my detective force. You may be useful, who knows?"

The words, designed merely to be comforting, were idly, kindly spoken, and carried little real weight. Had the master of the house really suspected how true they were to prove he would have been astonished.

CHAPTER VIII

A BLUNDER AND WHAT CAME OF IT

As if a weight had been removed from his soul Walter moved away. The whole world had suddenly become a different place. Although the calamity of Lola's disappearance was none the less distressing at least on his own particular horizon there no longer loomed the spectre of discharge and all the disgrace that accompanied it. He could have tossed his cap into the air for very joy and gratitude. In his relief he was bursting to talk to somebody, and as he had permission to use the telephone in order to keep in touch with his family it occurred to him that now was the moment to call up Bob and impart the exciting tidings of the afternoon. Bob was always off duty at this hour and if he had the good luck to find him at the station just the sound of his voice would be infinitely comforting.

Hastening in the side door he glanced into the wee telephone closet.

No one was there, and he took down the receiver and called the Seaver Bay station. In another instant Bob's *Hello* came cheerily over the wire.

"It's Walter, Bob."

"Anything the matter, kid?"

"N—o. Yes. That is, something *was* the matter but it is all over now. I just wanted to talk to you."

"Well, fire ahead. What do you want to say?"

"Oh, a lot. I hardly know how to start." The boy laughed nervously.

"You're not sick?"

"Oh, no."

"Well, we can't hold this line forever, son, so break away and tell your tale as fast as you can."

"I'll try to, Bob."

Incoherently the lad poured out his story. Once launched it came readily from his tongue and he continued to the end of it without interruption from his distant listener. When, however, he had finished, Bob's crisp tones came singing over the wire:

"You went out to walk about three, you say?"

"Yes."

"And returned?"

"It must have been half-past four or five, I guess."

"And there was nobody about the place all that time?"

"The men were all busy somewhere else. Strangely enough even Jerry, who usually is on deck, had a telephone call and had to go up to the big house."

"Oh, he did!"

"Yes. It was funny, too, because it was somebody he didn't know at all and he couldn't find out what the fellow wanted."

"What's that?" The interrogation was sharp and tense.

"Jerry just said it was some man up in Brockton whom he didn't know and as he couldn't make head nor tail out of the message he hung up the receiver. Nobody ever telephones to Jerry. It was queer they should do it to-day, wasn't it?"

"Very. Did you tell Mr. Crowninshield about it?"

"Oh, no, indeed. He was too busy about Lola to think of anything else."

"Nevertheless, I would tell him."

"What for? It wouldn't interest him."

"I think it might—a good deal. You tell him. Do you know whether he has done anything yet or not?"

"No, I don't. I didn't dare ask him what he was going to do."

"I suppose not. Well, I'm glad you got out of this snarl so well, kid. It's a pity they've lost the dog. You take mighty good care of the rest of the pups and don't let any more of them disappear."

"I'll try. And Bob——"

"I can't stop to talk any longer now, old chap. So long! If they get a line on the thief you might ring me up again. I shall be interested. Good-by."

"Good-by, Bob."

How fair Bob always was, reflected the boy, as he emerged into the open and made his way back to the kennels. Some brothers would probably have blurted out, "That's you all over!" or "Trust you to get into a mess!" But Bob never enjoyed seeing somebody else miserable. Instead he always tried to make everybody's troubles smaller than they really were. One could confess one's sins to Bob, knowing that he would be merciful.

So thought Walter as he sped down the gravel path to greet the clamoring pack of animals that hungrily awaited his coming.

"Well, old sports!" called he as he turned the key in the lock, "I guess you are ready for your supper. Wondering where your boss was, eh? I'm not very late. Only a quarter of an hour. It isn't late enough to warrant your making such a fuss. Down, Achilles! What's the matter with you? Anybody'd think you were crazy to see you jumping up and whining this way. What's got you, old man? Down, I say!"

He pushed the dog from him and started to enter the room where the food was kept; but again Achilles was in his path.

"Get out of my way, you beggar!" smiled Walter, playfully attempting to shake the creature off. "What is it? Are you clean starved? If you are you must stand out of the way so I can get you something to eat."

But the dog refused to move.

Planting himself squarely in the lad's pathway he began to bark furiously.

Then he raced to the gate, sniffed, and struggled to get out.

"What on earth has struck you, you giant?" inquired Walter, regarding the great creature in bewilderment. "Don't you want your dinner?"

It was plain in an instant that no matter what the lure of a bone might ordinarily be, to-day it held no charms for the big police dog. He had one wish and only one, and that was to be released from the wire enclosure in which he was penned and left free to follow some plan of his own which evidently absorbed him. So insistent was his demand that it was not to be denied and Walter slipped the bolt and allowed him to race away. Then the boy turned his attention to feeding the other dogs.

"Achilles probably has a bone buried somewhere," he muttered to himself, "and is going to dig it up. Just why he prefers stale food to fresh I can't see; but apparently he does."

Nevertheless His Highness had scarcely finished giving the dogs their dinner before Achilles was back again, and with no bone, either. On the contrary he was hot, breathless, and panting from what had obviously been a long run through the woods. Pine needles clinging to his furry coat attested that he had been over in the grove that flanked the estate on the west.

"Couldn't find your hidden treasure, eh, old boy?" commented Walter. "Gone, was it? Some other dog taken it?"

But Achilles failed to accept the jest with the cordiality such jokes commonly evoked. He neither wagged his tail nor stretched his jaws into a grin. Instead he began to yelp and bound back and forth upon the lawn.

"You act possessed. What on earth is the matter?" asked the boy, coming toward the gate and starting to open it.

No sooner was his hand on the latch, however, than the Belgian raced up with sharp barks of delight.

"Want me to come out, do you? Got something to show me?"

Again Achilles barked joyfully.

"Aren't you the tyrant, though?" remarked Walter. "I've just been for a walk and am tired as the deuce. What do I wish to go tramping over the country again for?"

Nevertheless, despite his grudging protest, nothing else would satisfy the dog and at length, curious to see what caused the creature's excitement, he slipped the lock and stepped outside on to the turf. Instantly an exultant bark came from Achilles and he dashed away, only to return and take the lead through the woods, his nose to the ground and his ears erect. The boy followed. It was a race to keep up with the rapidly running vanguard. Now the chase skirted the lawn, now dipped into the pine woods. On and on went the dog, and in pursuit of him on and on went Walter.

They floundered along the slippery matting of copper, stumbling this way and that, and presently emerged where the land dropped down to the shore. The lad paused. He had no mind to scramble through the tall salt grass or sink ankle deep in the stretch of sand that adjoined it. But Achilles compelled. It was now no longer a matter of choice. The beast approached and catching the corner of the lad's sweater in his mouth tugged at it resolutely, even angrily.

Walter dared not resist. He let himself down over the edge

of the bank into the sharp-edged grass, and wading through it reached the sand. Here Achilles halted. The end of their pilgrimage had, then, been reached. What was it all about? For a moment dog and man faced one another. Then, glancing about, His Highness gave a little cry. There were footprints in the sand,—deep footprints that the moisture had kept indelible. A train of them came and went toward a ribbon of automobile tracks that narrowed away up the beach and were finally lost in the confusion of a much traveled wood road.

Walter's heart leaped within him as the significance of the discovery rose before his imagination. This was the way Lola had gone.

A thief, familiar with the country and knowing the isolation of this sequestered cove, had driven through the wood road, left the car behind the dunes, and skulking through the woods, had successfully carried out a daring robbery. Perhaps he had been lingering concealed about the gardens all day or even many days. Who could tell? At any rate, he had chosen a propitious moment, provided himself with a skeleton key, and carried Lola away in the waiting motor car. Where they were now, who could tell? A car travels fast and a long distance could be covered in the two hours that had elapsed. Certainly no more time must be wasted.

With Achilles leaping before him Walter raced back to Surfside. Mr. Crowninshield, irritable and excited, was just coming out of the house.

"May I speak to you a moment, sir?" panted the boy.

"Yes, if it is important. I'm in a rush so do not delay me."

"But it's about Lola."

"Lola! Go ahead, then, if you have anything to say."

The lad told his story.

"Ha! Well done, Achilles!" exclaimed the financier when the tale was told. "Well done, old fellow! And well done you too, little shaver! Between you you have given us a big boost toward catching the thief. Now just one thing, sonny. I meant to caution you before you left but forgot it. You are not to speak of this affair to any one—not to any one at all. Do you understand? A false move on our part might undo everything and ruin our cause. Nobody is going to be caught red-handed with that dog in his possession. Rather than be trapped he would kill her. We mustn't let that happen. We shall follow up our man quietly without letting him suspect that he is being watched. That is the only way we can hope to get the pup back again. So mind you hold your tongue. Not a word to anybody on your life. Not a syllable. Be dumb as the grave and let me see how capable you are of keeping your own counsel. The trouble with most people is they blab everything. They can't wait to tell it. Let anything happen and they are off to confide it to some one before you can say Jack Robinson. Now don't you do that—at least not this time. Hold your tongue. This isn't your secret; it's mine."

In terror Walter hung his head. Should he confess that he had already telephoned Bob or should he keep silent.

Of course Bob wouldn't tell. There wouldn't be anybody to tell way off there at Seaver Bay. Besides, he himself could ring him up and caution him not to. Why need Mr. Crowninshield know anything about it?

But suppose Bob had told already and harm was done? Certainly it would be more honest to speak.

The boy took a big swallow.

"I'm afraid, sir, that I have already told some one," he blurted out miserably. "I didn't know it would do any harm and so I called up my brother and——"

"You young idiot!" burst out Mr. Crowninshield indignantly. "Why in thunder couldn't you keep still? We're in a nice mess now! If the story gets about and the police start to track down the thief it is good-by to Lola. Why did you have to run hot-footed to the telephone the first thing? Jove!"

"I'm very sorry, sir. I had no idea it would do any harm."

"But you have an idea of it now, haven't you?" inquired the master grimly.

"Yes. I see what you mean."

Mr. Crowninshield heaved an exasperated sigh.

"The game's up now, I guess," he muttered.

"But my brother lives off by himself in a very lonely place," the lad explained desperately. "Just he and another fellow have a house out on a point of land a long way off from everywhere. They couldn't tell anybody about Lola if they wanted to, especially if I call them right up and ask them not to."

"Where is it?"

"Seaver Bay."

"Never heard of it—or, stop a minute, isn't there a wireless station there or something?"

"Yes, sir. My brother——"

"Well, no matter about your brother now. You go into the house and call him up. When you get the line let me know and I will speak with him."

"Yes, sir." Nevertheless the lad lingered. "I'm—I'm awfully sorry," repeated he.

"There, there, go along. You meant no harm. You just blundered. But blunders are expensive things sometimes and this one may prove so unless we can prevent it."

Still His Highness did not go.

"Well, what are you waiting for?" asked his employer impatiently.

"My brother told me to tell you that Jerry had a telephone message this afternoon."

"A telephone message? What has that got to do with it?" burst out Mr. Crowninshield at the end of his patience.

"I don't know. Bob just said to tell you."

"Go ahead then."

Hurriedly the boy related the facts of the mysterious communication.

"So! Your brother has some brains if you haven't," said Mr. Crowninshield on hearing the story, and Walter saw him smile. "That was neat of them, very! They took the precaution to get Jerry, who is unfailingly about, out of the way."

"They?"

"The thieves, youngster. It was a Brockton call, you say."

"That was what Jerry told me."

"Good! That gives us another clue."

It was evident the information had put the master in rare good humor.

"Trot along, now, and call up this brother of yours. I shall be glad to talk with him, for he sounds as if he might be worth talking to. As for you, son, cheer up! No milk is spilled yet and perhaps it won't be if you have as wise a big brother as it appears. I might never have known of Jerry's message but for him. Jerry himself would not have placed enough importance on it to tell me, I am sure—or you, either, for that matter. So perhaps, after all, you did a good thing to enlist your brother in our behalf."

"I hope so, sir. I meant no harm; really I didn't."

"There, there, don't think of it again," said Mr. Crowninshield kindly. "I should have remembered you are not a man's age and cannot be expected to have the judgment that goes with fifty or sixty years of living. Even old codgers like myself blunder sometimes."

His eyes twinkled and in the radiance of his smile Walter saw the last cloud of wrath roll from his brow. Truly, as Jerry had affirmed, Mr. Crowninshield's rages were like thunderstorms—awesome while they lasted but unfailingly followed by sunshine.

CHAPTER IX

MORE CLUES

Notwithstanding Mr. Crowninshield's comforting words, however, Walter could not shake off the consciousness that take it all in all he had blundered desperately throughout the entire train of events connected with Lola and his vanity was sadly hurt. If any good had come out of what he had done it was more by chance than as a result of wise calculation. He had meant well, that was all that could be said, and the patronage these words implied was by no means flattering to one anxious to make himself valuable to his employer.

What a boob he was; what a blunderer! The name Mr. Crowninshield had so wrathfully bestowed on him was unquestionably deserved. It fitted him like a glove. The fact that the great man had afterward sought to palliate the sting of the term did not actually help matters any. What he had thought in the beginning and so spontaneously declared was what he really believed, and as his dispirited retainer observed to himself, who could blame him?

He couldn't have made a worse start at a job had he tried. In his depression he almost wished he had never seen Surfside, the Crowninshields, or anything belonging to them.

Nor was his melancholy lightened when he found on entering the house that the telephone line was busy and that some one was calling Mr. Crowninshield. Goodness only knew how long it might be now before the wire would be free for the master to reach and warn Bob to keep secret the tidings his brother had tattled to him. Wasn't it infernal luck to encounter this delay? If he had only held his tongue in the first place! Well, it had taught him a lesson. The next time he got mixed up in somebody else's affairs he would keep them to himself.

Meandering aimlessly outdoors he sat down on the steps to wait until the owner of the house should finish his conversation.

For a time he remained quite quiet; but when the minutes lengthened into a quarter of an hour he began to fidget. Would the talkers never stop? Why, their chattering seemed to be endless? Even through the door he could hear Mr. Crowninshield's curt tones and the eager rise and fall of his voice. Once he laughed as if pleased, and twice Walter heard a cry of "*Good!*" When he did appear on the piazza his face was wreathed in smiles.

"That brother of yours is a Jim Dandy!" he exclaimed, rubbing his hands. "You did a mighty clever thing, young one, to get him on the job. We never can thank you enough."

"Me?"

"Certainly you! Why didn't you tell me more about this family paragon of yours? I didn't take in he was a radio operator."

"I—I—I don't know," replied Walter, bewildered.

"Well, his quick action has helped us no end—that is all I can say," announced the owner of Surfside triumphantly. "The instant he got your message he went to work with his wireless outfit. He flashed messages to all the stations in the outlying cities or else telephoned, and inside of half an hour every road to Boston and to New York was watched. You see a man with a little dog had stopped at his station for water. The wood road skirting our shore goes right by Seaver Bay and probably the thief reasoned that no one would be on the lookout for him on such an out-of-the-way thoroughfare. At any rate he had to have water for his engine and he took a chance. He told your brother he was touring the Cape, and had you not called Bob up he would have thought no more of the happening. But when you told him about Lola immediately he pricked up his ears. The dog tallied perfectly with what you had previously told him and the fact that it was a Pekingese made him suspicious. Leaping at the possibility that his visitor was in reality the man wanted, he sent out a broadcast describing the culprit.

"With an accurate description of the man, car, and dog we cannot fail to get tidings soon. And at any rate we have something definite to work on. We know what the thief looks like, what he had on, the make of his car and all about him. Unquestionably he will be stopped either between here and Boston or between here and New York,—for he is probably aiming for one of those cities. I myself rather think he will go straight through to Boston. He would not venture to try New York until later because he would be well aware that the authorities there would be waiting for him. He isn't going to be trapped. So he will try to do the thing he figures I will not calculate upon." Mr. Crowninshield rubbed his hands and laughed. "Little does he know we have him down cold already! And it has all been so quietly and promptly done. That is the beauty of it. You must have got home from your walk very soon after the wretch had left. Therefore the loss was discovered sooner than he had planned. Doubtless he was delayed by Jerry's being about and had to wait until his accomplice up in Brockton called him off. I presume they had agreed upon some hour when they would summon the unsuspecting caretaker to the telephone." As the scheme of the robbery began to unfold, Walter mirrored his employer's smile.

"And if the other chap is in Brockton doesn't that indicate that this fellow who was here will most likely expect to pass through there and pick him up?" he ventured, feeling very much of a personage to be thus taken into Mr. Crowninshield's confidence.

"Exactly!"

His Highness glowed with satisfaction. Some of his self-esteem was returning.

"Fortunately your brother had the good sense to warn his allies to act carefully and not alarm the thief, so that the life of the dog might not be jeopardized. He seems to have thought of everything, this brother Bob of yours. If we get Lola back it will be largely his doing—and yours. I sha'n't forget the fact, either."

Walter flushed under the great man's praise.

"It was just a happen," murmured he. "I thought I had blundered."

He saw Mr. Crowninshield color at having his own word hurled back at him.

"Some of the most fortunate strokes in our lives are achieved by chance," replied he, laughing. "See how capable I am of shifting my philosophy," he added with good humor. "Nevertheless, although this indiscretion of yours has turned out well I still maintain that, generally speaking, a silent tongue is a great asset. In nine cases out of ten keeping still does far less harm than talking. Jerry is a shining example of my creed. In all the years he has been here he has never let his tongue outrun his solid judgment. And yet," concluded he with a twinkle, "had we trusted to Jerry, we should never have heard of his Brockton telephone communication. So there you are! Which is the better way? It seems to be a toss up in this case."

"I guess the better way is never to make a mistake," smiled Walter.

"Do you know the infallible person who can boast such a record?" came whimsically from Mr. Crowninshield.

"N—o, sir."

"Nor I."

A pause fell between them and Walter rose to go.

"Do you suppose you will hear anything more to-night?" questioned he shyly.

"There is no telling. We may have news at any moment; or again we may hear nothing until into the night or till morning."

"I'm crazy to get tidings, aren't you?" In his earnestness the lad had forgotten that they were not of an age or quite of the same station.

The master smiled indulgently.

"I'm every bit as crazy to hear as you are," said he, quite as if Lola were their joint possession.

"Do you think you'll get any message before I go to bed?"

Once more Mr. Crowninshield regarded him with friendly comradeship.

"That depends on what time you turn in."

"At home Ma makes me go at nine o'clock. I've done it pretty much, too, since I've been here. She wanted I should."

"You are a sensible fellow. Nine o'clock is late enough for any-body to sit up, although I will admit," the man chuckled mischievously, "that in New York we occasionally sit up later than that."

But Walter ignored the jest.

"Do you think you will hear by nine?" persisted he.

"There is no way of knowing, sonny," was the kind answer. "The best thing for you to do, however, is to go to bed as you usually do. You are tired out with excitement. I can see that."

"No I'm not," contradicted the boy, his eyes very wide open.

"But you are—a deal more fagged than you realize. I am myself. Now I'll tell you what we'll do. I'll go to bed and you go to bed; and if any message comes I'll tell them to waken me and then I'll waken you. I can call you on the wire that goes from the house down to your quarters. How will that do?"

"But suppose I shouldn't hear it?" objected the lad.

"Somebody will. The chauffeurs do not go to sleep as early as you do, I rather fancy. I will give orders for one of them to tell you if a call comes."

"I'd much prefer to sit up, sir. Why couldn't I just sit here on the piazza? It wouldn't disturb anybody and I should be on the spot."

"You might sit here all night and catch your death of cold, and no tidings come until morning, sonny. No, my plan is much the better one. You trot along to bed. I'll fulfill my part of the contract and go also. And if there is anything to tell before morning you shall hear it."

Reluctantly the lad moved away.

He was not in the least sleepy. Nevertheless because he had given his word he dragged himself across the lawn, mounted the stairs to his room, and began to undress. His spirits were very high. Within an hour or two—three hours at the very most—the telephone would ring and Mr. Crowninshield would announce to him the glad tidings that the thief had been caught. Then some one would motor to Barnstable, Brockton, or wherever it was, recapture Lola, and bring her back, and the events of the past few hours would be only a nightmare. And it would be Bob—he and Bob—who brought about this glorious climax to a day of catastrophes. And if such a result was accomplished had not the owner of Surfside promised that he would never forget the service?

For his own part Walter wanted nothing. If Lola could only be found his happiness would be complete. But if only Mr. Crowninshield would do something wonderful for Bob! Perhaps he might give him a big sum of money; he could well afford to. Or maybe he would put him in the way of earning it. There was no telling what Aladdin-like feats he might perform. Such a man was all powerful. Why, he could send Bob to Europe if he chose! Or pay the mortgage on the house. He could make Bob's fortune.

The younger boy thrilled at the thought.

With these optimistic and intriguing fancies in mind he slipped into bed and soon dozed off into dreams wilder and even more extravagant. He slept soundly and awoke with a bewildered cry when a knock came at the door.

"It's I—Wheeler, shaver! The boss wants you on the telephone."

Up scrambled Walter, his stupor banished by the agitation of the moment.

He did not wait to don his clothes but in his pajamas took the stairs two at a time and soon had his ear to the receiver.

"Walter?"

"Yes, sir."

"Well, we have some news, such as it is." Mr. Crowninshield's voice sounded dubious and discouraged. "They tracked the car we were after to Buzzard's Bay and found it there empty; its occupants had disappeared."

"Disappeared!" repeated the astounded boy.

"Yes, they're gone! Vanished in thin air! Not a trace of them is to be found. The abandoned automobile with its number removed, was discovered on a side road."

"The man must be hiding somewhere in the vicinity then."

"That does not follow, son; I wish it did."

"What else could he do?"

"His accomplice from Brockton could meet him with another car, for one thing."

"A different car, and throw us off the scent!"

"Precisely."

For a second neither of them spoke. Walter was too nonplussed and his employer too disheartened.

"Isn't that the limit!" the lad presently gathered indignation enough to ejaculate.

"I expected something of the sort," was the reply. "We are up against professionals, you see, and not amateurs. This gang is being paid big money and does not intend either to fail in what it has undertaken or be trapped. We had it too easy at the beginning and were too much elated by our initial success."

"What are you going to do now?"

"I've wired New York for detectives. I ought to have followed my first impulse and done it immediately, and I should have had we not seemed on the high road to success without help. The plain-clothes men will probably be miffed at being called in now that we have meddled with the case and messed it all up."

"But I don't see how we have done any harm," retorted His Highness, feeling it a little ungrateful of Mr. Crowninshield to veer so quickly from commendation to censure.

"Oh, untrained people never can compete with skilled ones in any line," was the sharp answer. "I ought to have remembered it. Doubtless in our zeal we betrayed ourselves somehow and our man became suspicious and adopted other tactics in consequence."

"I don't believe so," Walter maintained stoutly. "I'll bet this is just what he had arranged to do anyway."

"Well, perhaps it was. We cannot tell about that," yawned the man at the other end of the wire. "The result, however, is the same. Instead of netting our catch we have allowed it to slip through our fingers."

There was an edge of exasperation in the tone.

"Maybe we'll have better luck than you think," ventured the lad, not knowing what else to say, and unwilling to betray his chagrin.

"We'll have neither good luck nor bad in future," responded the master curtly. "After this we keep our hands off and the detectives manage the affair. There have been blunders enough."

With this ungracious comment the great man hung up the receiver and stumbling through the darkness His Highness felt his way upstairs and dropped into bed.

Like a house of cards his roseate dreams for the future had suddenly collapsed. There would be now no wonderful career for Bob, no bag of gold, no fairy fortune! Instead of being a hero he had again become a mere duffer, a blunderer, had played the fool.

Since failure had come in place of the coveted success Mr. Crowninshield would most likely blame it all to him.

Fleeting, indeed, was the favor and gratitude of princes!

CHAPTER X

BOB

By late afternoon of the following day the New York detectives arrived and Wheeler drove their dusty and travel-stained car around to the garage.

"Must have speeded up some!" commented he, on viewing the throbbing machine. "Left New York at midnight," they said. "Some friends of the master's likely, come to play golf."

Ever given to frankness it was on the tip of Walter's tongue to declare the real identity of the strangers, but fortunately he bethought him in time to halt the words.

"What did they look like?" inquired he, eager to know and yet anxious not to appear inquisitive.

"Look like? Like any other dusty, muddy guys," grumbled Wheeler, eyeing with disdain the grimy automobile which he knew he would be expected to clean.

"Old or young?" persisted His Highness.

"Old enough to know better than to heat up an engine this way, but young enough to do it," snapped Wheeler. "Shouldn't think their car had seen water in years, it's that filthy. A rum job for me!"

Walter, however, did not reply. He was not in the least interested in the mud-caked car. It was its occupants that aroused his curiosity. In all his life he had never seen a genuine detective and he was all impatience for a peep at persons allied with such an intriguing profession. While his reason told him they must, of course, look precisely like other men, nevertheless the hope would persist that perhaps, after all, they didn't. And even if they did appear like ordinary mortals were there not their myriad disguises? He hoped with all his heart they would wear some of these, that the exigencies of the case would compel it.

Very great, then, was his surprise and disappointment when on being summoned to the big house soon after the arrival of these interesting creatures he was presented to two common-place beings who, although charming gentlemen, were not in the least different from anybody else. Mr. Dacie, the younger of the men, was a pleasant, blond-haired fellow who instantly ingratiated himself in the boy's affections by asking him if he collected stamps and bestowing on him two rare ones from China. In fact he seemed to like everything a boy liked and appeared to be almost a boy himself.

Mr. Lyman was older but he, too, when he was not being stern and business-like, was very jolly. No one could possibly be afraid of either one of them and then and there His High-ness's faith in the ultimate success of Mr. Crowninshield's cause dwindled and died. They weren't disguised at all; and if they had pistols they must have had them well concealed for the only suspicious articles produced from their pockets were notebooks and pencils. He had expected to be quite awed by their presence but on the contrary he found, when he started out to show them the kennels and the place where he had seen the automobile tracks, that he was chattering away to both of them quite as if he had known them all his life.

Mr. Dacie was particularly friendly, and as they walked along he talked much of sports, dogs, and fishing. Furthermore he was intensely interested in Bob and listened attentively to all that was told him about this remarkable big brother. He had a bully brother himself, he said. In short, before a half hour had passed His Highness had not only decided to become a detective but to become one exactly like Mr. Dacie.

And yet as he thought it over afterward the hero of his sudden adoration had not uttered one syllable about jails, criminals, robberies, or crimes of any sort. In fact he had talked really very little. What he had done had been to smile, nod, and let the other fellow babble. It had, to be sure, been a delightful experience to find yourself a lion, and everything you did of interest to your listener; but you did not learn much about the business of being a detective, reflected Walter, a bit mortified by his discovery. Well, the next time he was with Mr. Dacie he would ask him some questions and let him relate everything about his mysterious calling.

Strange to say, however, the moment for such disclosures never appeared to come right. There was always so much else to talk of. Mr. Dacie wanted most terribly to catch some flounders and wondered if there were any to be found; and of course as Walter knew of three secret places where flounders were sure to lurk he eagerly told his new friend about them. And then he had to talk swimming and school—and how he hated it! Why, there were endless things to tell Mr. Dacie. The visit of the two men was, moreover, surprisingly short. They remained at Surfside only one night and the next morning, together with Mr. Crowninshield, who led the way in his car, they disappeared leaving His Highness none the wiser and regretfully mourning his lost opportunity to be initiated into the gruesome mysteries of a detective's career.

The realization that in exchange for telling everything he

knew or ever had thought Mr. Dacie had told him nothing suddenly caused the lad to speculate as to whether after all both Mr. Dacie and his associate, Mr. Lyman, were not cleverer than they looked to be.

It seemed incredible to recall, now that they were gone, that he had not once asked them what they thought about Lola and whether they had any idea where the man who had taken her had gone. How much better it would have been had he made that inquiry instead of chattering about his own affairs. But somehow when there had been a lull in the conversation they had always been busy measuring footprints or automobile ruts, and writing down these unending dimensions. Moreover, something which he was unable to explain always halted the questions.

Well, it was useless to regret his vanished opportunities. The detectives were now far beyond his reach and probably he would never see them again. He might as well go about his work and put them, together with Lola and her baffling disappearance, out of his mind. This he tried valiantly to do, but in spite of his utmost endeavor his thought constantly reverted to the missing dog, and when toward dusk Mr. Crowninshield's car came whirling up the avenue His Highness had all he could do not to rush out and demand of the master whether he had secured any further information.

To remember that he must keep constantly in the background was, in fact, one of the most difficult aspects of Walter's job. As a democratic young American who had always mingled in the best society Lovell's Harbor had to offer he had been free to give a hail to anybody he desired to greet. But at Surfside everything was different. He must stifle his natural impulses and curb his tongue, a role very hard for one who had had no previous experience with class distinctions. Difficult as it had been he had made up his mind to being excluded from the gayety that went on about him. It was, to be sure, no fun to view automobile loads of young people roll out of the drive bent on a day of pleasure; to look on while motor boats pulled up anchor and puffed across the blue of the bay. And how he would have adored to try his hand at a set of tennis on that fine dirt court! Ah, there were moments when to a normal, healthy boy the world appeared a very unfair place; and the lot of one who worked for a living a wretched one.

And then, when his spirits had reached their lowest ebb, he would resolutely take himself to task. Was there not his pay envelope to compensate him? He was not at Surfside to have a good time; he was there to earn his daily bread and very fortunate was he to have so good a place. Having read himself this lecture he was wont to turn to his duties with lighter heart, closing his ears to the laughter and his eyes to the merriment that made up the days of the idle. But what he never could get used to was the fact that he must not ask questions or voice his opinions. In a free country where one man was as good as another the mandate seemed absurd. But it wasn't done. That was all there was about it. Jerry said so and so did Tim.

Instead of piping, "Hi, Mr. Crowninshield, did you find out anything?" one awaited the information until it was voluntarily imparted.

In this particular case, as good fortune would have it, His Highness's impatience had seethed and bubbled only a half hour before who should come strolling down to the kennels but the very gentleman the lad was feverish to interrogate.

Arrayed in a cool Palm Beach suit and a soft hat of white felt he sauntered up as indifferently as if the boy's curiosity were not at the boiling point and said, "Good evening," in a perfectly calm, self-possessed tone.

"Good evening, sir," Walter replied.

"Dogs all right?"

"Yes, sir."

"No more of them missing?"

"Not on your—no, sir."

The great man turned away to conceal a smile.

"I've been seeing your brother to-day," remarked he.

"Bob?"

Mr. Crowninshield nodded.

"Yes. We went over to the Seaver Bay wireless station."

The lad waited.

"You have a very fine brother, youngster, and one whom you may well be proud of."

"Yes, sir."

(What was the use of telling him that? His Highness knew what a corker Bob was without being told. Much better tell him what had happened at Seaver Bay, what the detectives said, and whether Lola had been found!)

"We had, in fact, quite a talk with your brother."

"Yes, sir." The reply came automatically.

"He was able to furnish us with much information regarding the man we are chasing up."

"Yes, sir."

"Yes," ruminated Mr. Crowninshield with evident satisfaction, "we have the thief sketched in quite clearly."

"Yes, sir."

"With the details your brother gave us Dacie and Lyman have a most encouraging foundation on which to work."

"Have they found out anything yet, sir?"

The question would out despite all Walter could do to stop it. He knew the instant it had left his tongue that he shouldn't have asked it and he stood there hot and embarrassed at his own audacity.

Much to his surprise, however, Mr. Crowninshield did not appear to be in the least offended. On the contrary he seemed pleased by the lad's eager interest and smiled at him kindly.

"Yes, we've found out something," said he, "but it is not very good news, I am sorry to say. Dacie and Lyman traced the car that carried Lola as far as Buzzard's Bay and discovered that there——"

"Yes?" interrupted Walter, so intent on the story that he was unconscious of interrupting.

"There," repeated Mr. Crowninshield, "the thieves embarked on a private yacht that awaited their coming; steamed through the Canal, and——"

"Don't say they are gone, sir!" cried the boy.

"I'm afraid so, sonny."

"Well, if that isn't the limit!"

"It is, indeed," rejoined the elder man heartily.

His Highness had staggered back against the door in consternation. If Mr. Crowninshield had affirmed that the thieves had taken flight in an aeroplane he could not have been more astonished than by the turn affairs had taken.

"What do you suppose they'll do now?" demanded he.

"We've no idea. They may make for New York, Boston, or some other port where they think they will be safe. There is no way of knowing. Or it may be that the person who hired them to get Lola is on the yacht and having now secured what he has been in search of he may simply cruise about and not land at all for months. Anything is possible."

"Could they get the name of the boat?"

"Yes, she's called the *Siren*."

"Then I should think it would be easy enough to track her down, board her, and bring Lola away," said Walter.

"It sounds simple, doesn't it?" Mr. Crowninshield returned. "But I am afraid it is not going to be as easy as that. We have no way of proving that Lola is aboard the yacht, in the first place. Moreover, even did we know that she was there, there are a thousand and one places where she could be hidden and defy discovery. And were the villains actually cornered nothing would be less difficult than to wring the puppie's neck and throw her overboard so that nothing would remain to identify the wretches with their crime."

"Scott!"

"You see now that to recover Lola is not such an easy matter."

"I'm afraid not, sir," was the dispirited response.

Mr. Crowninshield glanced at the dejected figure before him.

"We mustn't give up beaten yet, however," affirmed he, struggling to be cheerful. "The game isn't up, you know. Dacie and Lyman are clever men and I have given them a free rein as to money. If there is anything to be done they ought to be able to accomplish it."

Nevertheless optimistic as the words were it was plain to see that Mr. Crowninshield was not really as sanguine as he would have Walter think. There was a pucker of annoyance about the corners of his mouth, and his eyes looked dull and discouraged. Say what he might His Highness knew without being told that deep down in his heart of hearts Lola's master had resigned himself to never seeing her again.

For a few seconds the capitalist lingered, musing. Then he broke the stillness, hurling a bomb into the air with the words:

"By the by, I have made your brother an offer. I've suggested that he leave Seaver Bay and come here. I am going to give Dick a radio set for his birthday and I should like the aid of an expert in rigging it up. Besides, last season I installed a wireless on my yacht and shall need some one to operate it. This Bob of yours is precisely the sort of chap I want."

"Oh, Mr. Crowninshield!" was all Walter could stammer.

"You'd like having him here then?"

"You bet your—yes, sir, I would," gasped His Highness, making a dash after his manners.

"That's good," remarked the financier, much amused. "I hope he'll decide to come. You must use your influence to persuade him."

This time Walter did not forget his etiquette.

"I will, sir," replied he meekly.

CHAPTER XI

THE DECISION

That night when his day's duties had been discharged and he was free, the first thing His Highness did was to pen a much blotted and somewhat incoherent note to Seaver Bay. Almost every sentence of it was underlined and some of the persuasive adjectives and verbs were even emphasized in red pencil. Certainly what the epistle lacked in neatness and beauty of appearance was compensated for in sincerity and earnestness. This document mailed and reinforced by an ardent appeal over the telephone, there was nothing to do but possess one's soul of patience until Bob decided what it was best for him to do.

To throw up a government job with practically assured employment for a private venture which might be of short duration seemed madness and the young radio man with his level head and sober judgment was not one to leap at a decision. Carefully he weighed the pros and cons and while he did so Walter, and even Mr. Crowninshield himself, fidgeted. His Highness would not have hesitated a moment; and that any one should do so appeared to him incomprehensible. As for the master of Surfside who was accustomed to having his business offers snapped up the instant they were made, the younger man's deliberation piqued his interest and respect as almost nothing else could have done. He had thought the terms suggested very generous and had expected them to be seized with avidity. It was something new to have a penniless youth waver as to whether to accept or reject them.

In the meantime while the days passed no tidings came from the New York detectives and the dwellers at Surfside were compelled to settle down to their customary routine and put Lola's disappearance out of their minds. Gardeners toiled, flowers blossomed, Jerry mugged about with his misty blue eyes following every seed that was planted, every turn the lawn mower made; they followed, too, what Walter was doing and saw to it that the dogs were well cared for and that his young protégé neglected nothing.

Walter saw little of Dick now, for the house was filled with guests and the place humming with laughter and the rush of unending sports and picnics. There were tennis tournaments, golf matches, swimming races, regattas when small fleets of knockabouts maneuvered in the bay. In the midst of such a whirl of merriment it taxed all one's forbearance to be nothing more than the boy who cared for the dogs.

On one particularly fine, bracing June morning after the lad had returned from a solitary cross-country tramp with Achilles and the rest of the pack, his lot seemed to him especially unenviable. There was evidently to be a ball game. College boys with crimson H's on their shirts; men with a blue Y; together with a group of short-sleeved players not yet honored with insignia from their universities were hurrying out to the lawn with bats, balls, and catcher's mitts.

"You must pitch for the Blues, Dabney," called one fellow to another.

"Who's going to catch for the Crimson team?" piped another.

"I choose to play for Yale," came shrilly from another man who was lounging across the grass in immaculate white flannels.

"Come on and help Harvard along, Cheever," put in a strident voice.

"Not on your sweet life!" bawled Cheever, with a vehemence that made everybody laugh. "Goodness knows she needs help; but I'm not going to be the one to offer it."

Again there was a good-humored shout from the bustling throng.

"I'll line up with Yale to beat you though," Cheever added with a chuckle.

"You can line up, you shrimp, but we're going to do the beating," retorted an ardent Harvard supporter.

So the banter went on while the nines were being organized.

At length, however, there was a shout of dismay.

"We're lacking one man," announced the captain of the Crimsons, with sudden consternation. "Haven't you another chap who can play, Dick?"

"Nobody, I'm afraid, unless you want to haul in some of the chauffeurs," Dick answered idly.

"Jove! That's hard luck. We've got to have a shortstop. What are we going to do?"

"Wasn't there a boy around here somewhere this morning with the dogs? It seems to me I saw somebody—a stocky little chap with a snub nose."

The description was not flattering and Walter winced.

"Oh, that was King, who has charge of the kennels," replied Dick quickly. "I'm afraid he hasn't come back with the bunch of poodles yet."

"Yes, he has. I saw him skulking round the garage just now. Can't we drum him up?"

"Sure, if you can find him."

"There he is!" cried Cheever. "I say, you master of the hounds, come on over here. We want you."

Blushing red His Highness approached the noisy group.

"Did you ever play baseball, kid?" inquired the captain of the Harvard team.

"I believe so—once or twice," answered Walter soberly.

"Want to come in with us as shortstop?"

"Sure!"

"I've a glove that will fit him," put in a man called Richardson.

With scant ceremony His Highness was hustled into it and before he sensed what he was doing he was yelling with the rest, and head over ears in as exciting a game of ball as he had ever participated in.

There were excellent players on both teams and the scoring ran so even that it was a toss-up who would win. From jest the game dropped into deadly earnestness.

"It's your turn at the bat, Stubby," asserted Richardson to Walter unceremoniously. "Now remember who you're playing for. Don't hand Yale the game if you can help it."

"I'll do my best," was the modest reply as the lad gripped the bat, then rubbed his hands in the dirt to make his hold more certain.

The pitcher twirled a ball.

"One strike!" droned the umpire.

Again the leather disc spun through the air.

"Two strikes," called the warning voice.

"Great Scott, Stubbie, look out. Don't waste strokes like that, you boob. Let the things go by if they don't suit you. You don't *have* to hit them."

Once more the ball spun through the air. A smart crack followed and up into the blue leaped the ball, defying the pursuit of catcher or baseman.

"Beat it into home plate, George!" coached the captain excitedly. "Move along, you fellows! It's a run for Stubbie! Slide in, Stubbie! Pick up your heels and sprint! Go it! Go it! Keep out of the way, you chaps. Hurray! Bully for you, kid! A beauty! *Harvard! Harvard! Harvard!* Rah, rah, rah! Rah, rah, rah! Rah, rah, rah, *Harvard!*" The familiar cheer echoed loud above the shouting.

"That lays them out! They're dead men!" cried Richardson triumphantly. "Where did you learn to play ball, young one?"

"It's no fair borrowing a professional," the Yale leader objected, trying to make a joke of his defeat.

"Jove, but that was a pretty hit!" Dick said quietly to Walter. "A peach!"

"You're all right son!" affirmed the Harvard catcher. "Any time you are out of a job I'll recommend you to the Braves."

A general laugh went up.

Altogether the morning was a glorious day of comradeship, nor did it lessen His Highness's happiness when he returned to his quarters to see disembarking from Mr. Crowninshield's motor car the familiar form of Bob.

"I brought your brother back from Seaver Bay with me," explained the financier. "It took him so long to make up his mind whether he'd come here or not that I went over there to-day to find out whether he was dead or alive."

Mr. Crowninshield was plainly enjoying Walter's amazement.

"And you've come to stay?" His Highness, all delight and confusion, contrived to stammer.

"So they tell me," Bob laughed.

He was a tall, handsome fellow with a grave mouth and

thoughtful brown eyes; and when he spoke it was in a voice low and pleasing to the ear.

"Oh, Bob and I have lots of secrets we haven't let you into, little chap," affirmed the master of Surfside gaily.

"I never was so surprised!" gasped Walter.

"We meant you should be. Your brother settled everything up over the telephone a day or two ago."

"But, Bob, I don't see how you managed to get away from Seaver Bay so soon. You said it would probably be weeks before they could act on your resignation, even should you send it in, and afterward they would have to find some one to take your place."

"Luck came my way," Bob replied. "The government was closing the Bell Reef station and they simply shifted the two men who were there over to our place."

"Did you and O'Connel both decide to leave?"

Bob's eyes twinkled.

"O'Connel has just answered an advertisement as operator aboard a private yacht," said he, exchanging a glance with Mr. Crowninshield. Evidently there was some jest between them that amused them vastly.

Curiously Walter looked from one to the other.

"Better tell him, Bob," murmured the New Yorker in a low tone.

"Why you see, kid, O'Connel had a chance to go as wireless man aboard the *Siren*."

"Not—not the yacht that has Lola on it!"

"The very same—at least we hope it has Lola."

"But—but—I don't understand," muttered His Highness as if dazed.

"Evidently, so far as we can make it out, the *Siren* passed through the Canal and not daring to land, cruised along the coast where she must have met with rough weather. Of course that is purely surmise on the detective's part. Anyhow, her radio operator broke his arm and had to be replaced by another man so they advertised for some one. Luckily Dacie saw the item in the want column of the New York paper and set O'Connel on the job. The arrangements have all been by letter through the general mail delivery of New York so we still have no notion as to where the *Siren* is. On Tuesday, however, O'Connel is to go over to New York, an agent is to meet him, and he is to be told where to go."

"And I suppose Mr. Dacie or Mr. Lyman will be on hand and go along too to nail their man!" cried the delighted Walter.

"Not so fast, son," returned Mr. Crowninshield. "We are not going to track them down so close and scare them off at the outset. No, we sha'n't send any one with O'Connel. He'll go and meet the agent and follow up directions precisely as if he knew nothing about Lola. With Bob here operating a wireless and O'Connel in constant communication with him, we will have all the inside information we're after. O'Connel can soon let us know where the yacht is; whether Lola is aboard of her; and exactly when and where the owners of the *Siren* are proposing to land. They can't make a move which we shall not know about in a flash. A pretty neat arrangement, I call it!" The New York magnate rubbed his hands together softly.

"Gee! Well, Mr. Lyman and Mr. Dacie have sure been busy!" was Walter's comment.

"You do not mention that I, too, have been busy," chuckled Mr. Crowninshield. "While you have been chasing the dogs over the fields and playing baseball," he winked at Bob, "I have been telephoning to the city for a radio set—a corking fine one—for Dick's birthday. Bob, here, is going to install it with the aid of some New York electricians. It should be all in place inside a few days. Then if O'Connel has any messages for us we shall be ready for him. In the meantime Bob is going to break in you youngsters so that you or Dick can listen in and get any news that may come when he is off duty or aboard the yacht. If those fellows who bagged Lola think themselves so all-fired clever they will find they are mistaken. I did not go into this game to be beaten." Mr. Crowninshield squared his jaw with bulldog resolution.

"Now you and Bob trot off and have a visit together. Show him where his quarters will be. There is a room beside you where Jerry says he can bunk," continued the master of the estate. "Until the apparatus arrives from New York there won't be much he can do, so you better take the chance to go home and see your mother to-night—both of you. By to-morrow or the next day at the latest the electricians should be here with their stuff. Then things will hum!"

With a jaunty wave of his hand Mr. Crowninshield wheeled about and Bob and Walter were left alone.

CHAPTER XII

LESSONS

The joy of Mrs. King when she was informed that both her sons were to be all summer at Surfside cannot be pictured.

"Why, it is like a dream or an answer to prayer!" ejaculated she. "Think of having you so near! Now were Bob to be electrocuted, I could get to him within half an hour."

The fact evidently caused her profound satisfaction and each of her sons laughed.

"I'm not planning to end my days by electrocution," smiled Bob.

"Few do plan to," was the grim retort. "But anyway, whether or no, it is wonderful to have you so close at hand. I shall feel as if I had a great prop behind me."

"I hope so, Mater," Bob said affectionately.

"I suppose you'll not have much time to be spending at home, though," mused the mother presently. "Your work, likely, will keep you busy."

"I expect it will, especially during the next fortnight," Bob answered. "There will be all the apparatus to set up and get into working order; and in addition the equipment aboard the yacht must be overhauled. I want both wireless outfits in perfect condition for much depends on their being trim and tight."

"It isn't probable you'll have much to handle that is important," declared Mrs. King. "It won't be like dealing with government messages or wrecks." The two boys exchanged a glance. Much as they wished to they dared not initiate their mother into the secrets of Surfside.

"You never can tell what messages you'll catch by wireless," Bob returned ambiguously. "Besides, Mr. Crowninshield intends to have some of his business relayed to him from New York."

"Oh!"

"I guess I shall find plenty to do," the elder boy remarked.

"Well, I reckon you will at that rate. But do be careful, won't you? And don't let Walter go dabbling with those evil wires."

"I'll look out for him."

The evasive answer did not, however, satisfy the woman.

"Surely you don't mean to start Walter in learning about wireless, do you?"

"I may give him a few lessons, yes."

"Now don't you do it," retorted Mrs. King in spirited protest. "He was always a blunderer and were he to go messing about with electrical currents I should not have a happy moment. It is bad enough to have one of you in constant danger without two."

"But it isn't dangerous," Walter interrupted.

"Much you know about it," declared his mother, wheeling on him with scorn. "What experience have you had with radio, pray?"

Meekly the lad closed his lips.

"I am going to give some lessons to Mr. Crowninshield's son, Mater, and it seemed to me it was a good chance for Walter to learn something, too," Bob responded gently. "Sometime the kid might find it useful to have such knowledge. You never can tell. Nothing we learn is ever wasted."

"No, I suppose not," was the grudging reply. "Well, just stand over him and see that he doesn't kill himself."

"I've no desire to have him killed."

"No more you have. Of course not," Mrs. King smiled. "But you know if there is any way of crossing the wires he'll do it. He's made that way. Still, unlucky as he is, I'd not care to lose him."

Fondly she beamed on the ill-starred Walter.

"I'll keep at his elbow, Mother," said Bob soothingly.

"I know you will. You were ever good to your brother." She patted the big fellow's hand. "And mind the pair of you come to see me when you can. You'll be busy, I know; but you mustn't forget your mother."

"We'll not do that," cried the boys in chorus.

Nevertheless in spite of the promise there were few opportunities during the next few days for either of them to go a-visiting. The New York electricians arrived and with them came aerials, generators, detectors, tuners, insulators, amplifiers, and all the hundred and one parts necessary for a perfectly equipped radio station. Mr. Crowninshield had indulged in no cheap outfit. On the contrary he had purchased the best there was to be had and as the coils of copper wire, glistening wire rope, and spotless porcelain insulators were unpacked Bob's eyes sparkled with anticipation. With the touch of a connoisseur he handled the materials, examining the quality of each. What was Greek to the others was familiar ground to him.

A low building adjoining the boathouse had been hurriedly constructed and it was here, where the new station was to be situated, that an interested audience congregated daily. Perched on an overturned packing case Mr. Crowninshield surveyed the installment of the novel toy which was not only to gratify

Dick's birthday longings but also, he hoped, bring to him the information he coveted concerning Lola.

Much as he knew about stocks and bonds he was as much of a novice in the presence of things electrical as were either his son or Walter King, and therefore to their avalanche of questions he added still others, gratefully accepting the information Bob offered with the eagerness of one who is not too superior to learn.

"What is that thing they are putting in place now?" inquired he. "And what is it for?"

"Oh, even I can answer that, Dad!" cried the delighted Dick. "That is the aerial or antenna and it catches the wireless waves as they travel through the air. The higher and longer it is the better, so far as messages are concerned—that is, within certain limits."

His father's eyes twinkled.

"Where did you pick up so much knowledge?" chuckled he.

"Bob told me."

"I'll be bound he did," sniffed the man. "I wasn't asking about the antenna, though. Green as I am I recognized that. It was that other wire that interested me."

"The lead in?" asked Bob quickly.

"I guess so, although I never was introduced to it by name before."

Everybody laughed at the naive reply.

"The lead in, sir, is the conductor that carries the wireless waves from the aerial into the house. The idea is not to have it too long. It must run as directly as possible and be very carefully insulated from any buildings, trees, or masts because of the current."

"I see. And that other thing?"

"That is the lightning arrester. It can be fastened inside or outside the station, as is most convenient; but it is compulsory to have it to satisfy the insurance companies. The antenna is secured to it and by means of a ground wire any electrical discharges will in a great measure pass off through the earth."

"Mater should see that," murmured Walter mischievously to Bob.

The elder brother nodded humorously.

"The ground helps a lot in radio work," continued he. "In fact were it not for good old Mother Earth furnishing her aid, we should have no wireless at all. One side of our circuit passes through the ground and the other half, which completes it, goes through the air between the aerials of the different stations. Therefore you can readily see that it is most important to make sure of a good earth connection. Often city water pipes are resorted to, the contact being made by soldering a wire to the water faucet. Down here on the Cape, however, where there are only wells and windmills we shall have to sink some metal plates in the ground and connect the wires with these."

"And that is all that goes outside the building?"

"Yes, sir. The lead in brings the wires into the station and they are then connected up with the receiver. Sometimes there are separate antennæ for sending and receiving messages. Of course the big stations always have two. But for a place this size and doing such a small amount of business we can send and receive from the same wire. With a tuner, which can be tuned to bring you into the same key with the station you are listening to, a detector to catch the signal after the persons talking have been brought into tune, and an amplifier that intensifies or increases the sound you have your receiving outfit. Batteries you know about without my telling you; and the head 'phones too, which you have of course seen telephone operators wear hundreds of times."

"Yes, I believe I should recognize one of those," laughed Mr. Crowninshield. "So that is all there is to it, eh?"

"That is about all there is to receiving, yes."

"The sending part of the machine is more complicated, is it?"

"Yes, sir. And so is the job," smiled Bob.

"I mean to learn to transmit as well as receive," put in Dick.

His Highness grinned derisively.

"Do you indeed!" said he. "Well, there is nothing like aiming high. But I guess for the present you'll be pretty well content if you get so you can take down the Morse code as it comes in."

"Is it so hard?"

"That depends on how good you are at memorizing dots and dashes. French verbs are nothing compared to it."

"I hadn't thought of learning to read code."

"You have to, son, if you are going into wireless. With a tutor here on the spot, it should not be difficult. Besides, that is half the fun. I want you to learn this thing intelligently and not just make a plaything of it. I've done my part by buying you the best outfit there was to be had. The rest is up to you."

"That's square, Dick," chimed in Walter.

"Sure it is. I'll go to it and do my darndest, too, Dad," returned the boy.

"That's the proper spirit!" exclaimed his father.

His Highness smiled with ironic satisfaction.

"If Bob is to tutor you you will study harder than you ever did in your precious life," whispered he. "I know Bob. He can be stiff as any college professor. He tutored me in Latin once to pull me through my exams and I barely lived. I don't envy you, old man."

"Gee! Will it be that bad?"

"You will get all the wireless coming to you, that's all. Take it from me," was the teasing rejoinder.

"Oh, I hope he won't bone down as hard as that," wailed Dick dolefully. "I want to get some sport out of this thing. I wasn't planning to be turned into a galley slave during hot weather."

Seeing that he had his victim thoroughly terrified Walter thought it time to shift the jest.

"Don't fret. I was only jollying, old chap," declared he. "Bob won't really stand over you with a whip. He is the best fellow alive. Still, he will expect you to work if you set out to do so. He is always terribly in earnest about whatever he undertakes. I suppose that is why he has got on so well and never failed to make a success of what he has tried to do. You can count on him to duff into this job with the same spirit. You'll get your money's worth of instruction, you may be sure, if he has been hired to give it."

Dick shrugged his shoulders.

"Well, I guess I can stand it if he is not too rough on me," responded he. "I do not mind studying so much if it is about a subject I like; and I am crazy about wireless."

"Oh, it isn't the wireless part I object to," drawled His Highness. "It is that dot and dash code that gets me. I never could learn it if I tried ten years; and as for taking twenty words a minute in any language—well, they could have the whole outfit before I'd do it."

"I shall be interested to see what speed I can make," mused Dick.

"Speed! You won't make any speed at all—at least not at first, so do not hope or expect to. If you even get the words correctly you will be going some," sniffed Walter. "Still, I guess you need

"YOU WILL GET ALL THE WIRELESS COMING TO YOU, THAT'S ALL.
TAKE IT FROM ME."

not worry for the present about receiving or sending messages for Bob will give you a lot to think about before that. As for the Morse code, you may not meet it for weeks."

"What do you mean?" Dick inquired.

"Oh, Bob will get right down to brass tacks at the start and find out what you know about electricity and wireless anyway. That is the way he did to me when he tutored me in Latin. He wasn't content with just translating Caesar but must needs splash right into Roman history and make me hunt up everything I could find about the Goths and the rest of those heathen tribes. Gee, but he made me sweat! He will do that with you and your wireless. If you think you are going to begin taking messages in code you don't know Bob."

Having delivered himself of these brotherly appreciations His Highness walked away, leaving Dick to ponder on the joyous prospects they contained. His sinister prediction Richard Crowninshield soon found to be true. Thorough was no name for Bob King. Before a week had passed Dick whimsically remarked to his father that it must be a task to Bob to swim on the top of the sea without diving down with a spy glass and examining every particle that was on the ocean's bottom. The fact that the new tutor never dipped into any subject but instead explored it greatly delighted Mr. Crowninshield.

"I shouldn't mind letting that young chap tutor me a little," observed he half jestingly to his wife. "I am as vague as a fog when it comes to this wireless business. I should get a lot of information if I listened in on Dick's lessons."

The words, idly spoken, much to the amusement of all became a reality. After drifting in to the first talk Mr. Crowninshield came to the second lesson and from then on he became a regular pupil.

"You needn't be afraid I have come here to criticize," explained he with appealing simplicity. "I'm green as grass and have come to learn."

"It is just that you have not had the time to take up radio, sir," was Bob's modest answer. "We all have our specialties."

"That's right," agreed the capitalist. "Sometimes I fall to wondering whether it is better to know something about everything or everything about something."

"To know something about everything would be spreading it pretty thin, I am afraid," was Bob's characteristic reply.

"That wouldn't do for you, eh?" remarked Mr. Crowninshield with a chuckle.

"It would not satisfy me; no, sir. As it is I cannot begin to master what there is to be known concerning this one branch of science. Were my head to be filled with a little of everything I should feel as if it were a grab bag."

"Many heads are," was the laughing retort. "Still, with each successive generation rolling up its accumulation of knowledge the intellectual snowball is getting to be of ponderous size. History's remedy for this malady has always been to knock the whole structure to pieces every now and then and begin again. Perhaps we shall have to have another period of the Dark Ages and another Renaissance to set us right."

Thoughtfully he puffed his cigar.

"This wireless now—think of the new fields it has opened up. Not only are our ships equipped so that they can send and receive all sorts of messages, get their location, be informed concerning harbor entrances and coast lines; set their compasses and clocks but soon wireless telephones will be installed in the staterooms of all passenger steamers so that those crossing the ocean can talk with their friends ashore any time they may elect to do so. Of course there are times when such a thing might have its advantages; but for tired people—doctors and the like—who are trying to get to a spot where they cannot be reached by business cares it will be a negative sort of blessing. I, myself, for example, always count on my stay on shipboard as a sort of vacation, an interval when nobody can bother me with office matters. But if in future I must have a wireless telephone at my bedside I shall be no more isolated than I should have been had I remained at home. Pretty soon there will be no place under the sun where a man can go and get peace and quiet. The Maine woods will be full of radio outfits and the tops of distant mountains in touch with the stock market. Even an aeroplane carries its wireless. It is hideous to contemplate!" he sighed. "As for city life, we shall be beset wherever we go. And if the fashion set by some of our city police of having wires tucked away in uniforms and a wireless receiver carried in the pocket prevails in due time even when we walk the streets we shall all be in constant touch with our particular headquarters."

At his rueful expression Bob could not but laugh.

"There certainly is no question that a great day for wireless is coming," replied he. "Whether we like it or not the thing has come to stay and as yet we have only half discovered what can be done with it. It is undoubtedly rough on those who want isolation. But most people don't. They are glad to feel, for instance, that the ocean is so small they can talk with their friends while they are crossing it. Besides, you must not forget how much good ship surgeons and doctors can now do for those who otherwise would have no aid at hand. Remote lighthouses and small ships that need medical service often signal the big liners now and ask advice of the ship's doctor. I heard a little while ago of a lighthouse keeper whose leg was amputated under the wireless direction of one of our great surgeons. Had instructions not been available the man would probably have died of blood poison. And many times there is sickness aboard small vessels that are out to sea. They signal the symptoms of their patients and the doctor hundreds of miles away replies with a remedy. As all boats carry medicine chests the distant physician can easily designate what dose to give."

"That is a fine idea!" nodded Mr. Crowninshield. "I hadn't thought of treating illness by radio. A bit tough on the doctor, though. It must keep him busy."

"I am afraid it does. In fact some of the ship's surgeons are demanding higher pay because of the rush of work put on them. To have the health of a large ship under one's supervision is task enough without treating all the people sailing the ocean. They say some doctors are all in after a trip simply because of the extra calls that pour in from outside ships and stations. It keeps them hopping day and night, for of course no decent doctor will ever refuse aid to those who are suffering."

"Humph! That is quite a new phase of wireless."

"It proves it can save life not only at a time of shipwreck but in other crises as well," Bob responded with enthusiasm. "Now all that remains is for some clever fellow to come along who shall find a remedy for the difficulties that baffle the radio man. Then the science will come into its own. We must get rid of static interference—our greatest bugbear."

"Come, come, son! You must not spring any of your technical terms on me. Remember that while I am old in years I am still young in radio knowledge. Before you go slipping those phrases jauntily off your tongue you have got to begin at the very beginning and tell us the laws on which the radio telephone is based."

"That is a rather big order, sir," Bob replied modestly. "However, I am willing to try to fill it. I can at least pass on to you all that I know myself."

"That will satisfy me," affirmed the capitalist. "I see no reason, either, why your young brother cannot arrange his work so that he can join our class. The more the merrier. I even propose to drag in my wife and daughter. If in future we are to have wireless apparatus wherever we go it will be unintelligent not to know something about it."

"I am afraid it is going to pursue us pretty much to every corner of the earth," smiled Bob gravely. "You see, one of its great advantages is that it can go where the telephone with its myriad wires and poles cannot. It would be out of the question, for example, to string telephone wires through densely wooded sections and to the tops of high mountains, and even if the impossible could be accomplished the expense of keeping such lines in proper repair would be so great that no one could afford to shoulder it. Poles rot and wires rust out with wear and exposure to weather. Then there is the damage from gales, ice-storms, and falling timber. Even under the best of conditions linemen would be kept busy all the time repairing the equipment. And as if these difficulties were not great enough in times of peace think of the added burden of protecting miles and miles of telephone wires in time of war. Contrast with this the small district to be protected when it comes to a wireless station. Instead of having soldiers scattered through miles of territory the few needed can be concentrated within easy reach of provisions and reinforcements. And the same advantages that the radio telephone has on land prevail as well at sea for transmission of messages by cable is a frightfully expensive thing. Not only is the laying of such a line difficult, dangerous, and costly, but to maintain it is expensive and hard as well. In time of war it is particularly at a disadvantage since the cable can be cut and all communication with the outside world easily severed. Wireless, on the other hand, is not dependent on any such extravagant equipment. It finds its own way through air, water, and earth with very little help from us; and if it has its defects we must not forget that the first telephones were far from perfect, and that both telephone and cable have also their disadvantages."

CHAPTER XIII

INFORMATION FROM A NEW SOURCE

During the interval when the new radio station was being put in order and the parts of the outfit assembled, Bob King and the two city electricians toiled early and late. They scarcely stopped to eat, so feverish was their haste. Mr. Crowninshield had let it be known that if the wireless apparatus was in condition to send and receive messages within a week he would add to the regular wages of the mechanics a generous bonus and this incentive was sufficient to cause the avaricious workmen to transgress the laws of the labor unions and forget any fatigue they may have experienced.

As for Bob he was far too eager to get into touch with O'Connel and the *Siren* to covet extra pay for rushing through the installment of the new service. A private signal had been agreed upon between him and his former associate and also an hour set when each day the operator aboard the yacht was to call him. O'Connel was to allow seven days for the work at Surfside to be finished and then his messages were to begin and both Mr. Crowninshield and his alert employee meant to be ready for him.

Hence Bob whipped on his helpers, using every ray of daylight that could be turned to the purpose and much of the night. Even after everything was placed and connected up there would yet remain a great deal of testing out and tinkering before the set would be in perfect working condition and it was for this delay he was preparing.

Much to his surprise, however, the parts went together with astonishingly little trouble. They had been well made and fitted perfectly. Everything needed was at hand and in consequence there was no sending to the city for materials and waiting until they could be shipped. Therefore as the allotted time sped by the job that accompanied it moved rapidly to its end.

"We are going to make it, sir," ejaculated Bob with shining eyes, beaming enthusiastically on the master of the estate. "She will be all set up and working by Saturday. That is the day O'Connel was to make his first try to get into communication with us. I can hardly wait to hear what he has to say."

"I am pretty anxious to know myself," returned the elder man. "If he can get a message through we should then find out where the yacht is and whether Lola is aboard her."

"I'm crazy to learn what has become of the villains who pinched the dog," added Bob. "Do you take it they are still cruising with the boat?"

"Oh, they must have been paid off and landed somewhere," was the answer. "There would be no sense in detaining the thieves on the ship until now. It would only mean paying them and having them to feed; besides one does not care to make two rascals members of a house party."

"You think they have escaped us then."

"If by escaping you mean getting to the city yes," nodded Mr. Crowninshield. "But I do not feel at all sure with Dacie and Lyman on their track that they will be entirely safe and unmolested in town. Those detectives are like bloodhounds and will run them down no matter where they may be hiding.

The mere fact that they have got to New York or Boston will not be much protection."

"You intend to get them then as well as to recover Lola."

"I certainly do," retorted Mr. Crowninshield with emphasis. "I am going to recover my property, jail the thieves, and bring the people who received the stolen goods to justice."

"They have a week's start of us," Bob observed doubtfully.

"But we have not been idle all that time, man, Dacie and Lyman have been working; O'Connel has been using his eyes and ears—I hope; and we have this wireless set up."

"Yes, we have certainly accomplished something," admitted Bob.

"Accomplished something! I should say we had! Besides, this is not the sort of case one need hurry on. Nothing is going to be done suddenly," explained the financier. "Having got the dog the people on the yacht will move at their leisure. They do not fear that any one is at their heels chasing them up. Furthermore the sea offers unending concealment for their crime should they be pursued and trapped. It is the thieves themselves who are the scapegoats and the ones in danger, according to their reckoning."

"I suppose so," agreed Bob. "Still, I cannot help wishing we might have got after them without even these few days intervening."

"You forget, my son, that our wireless is going to cover space so quickly that hereafter we shall have our information very quickly and shall be exactly as well off as most detectives used to be in double the time."

"Yes, that is so."

"Once we are in touch with O'Connel we can know every thought they think aboard the *Siren* as soon as they have thought it."

The uncertainties that clouded the younger man's face vanished.

"That's right," smiled he. "From now on we should be able to checkmate them pretty neatly."

Mr. Crowninshield put his finger to his lips significantly. The two city electricians were approaching.

"Well, sir," began the foreman, "I guess your wireless tests out pretty near right; we've signalled our home company and got a reply from New York clear as a bell. With this chap at hand," he motioned to Bob, "you won't be needing us much longer, I reckon."

"Have you got to rush back to another job?" questioned the financier.

"Well, there is always plenty to do," grinned the man good-humoredly.

"You couldn't remain over a few days and overhaul my yacht, could you? She is anchored out in the bay close at hand. If you could be tightening things aboard her and seeing everything is right I would keep this young man at this shore station."

"Why—" the mechanic hesitated, fingering the roll of bills that stuffed his pocket. "Why," repeated he, "I imagine we could fix things up with the boss and stick round until whatever you wanted done was completed, sir."

"Arrange it then. Get the yacht into condition quickly so we can put to sea any day now that we choose."

"We'll do that, Mr. Crowninshield," responded the men in chorus. "Unless there is a lot to do to the outfit—"

"There isn't. It was all new in the fall; and we have been in Florida this winter too, so the ship has been in commission and constantly taken care of."

"In that case there will probably be little repairing," nodded the spokesman. "Maybe tightening and oiling, and a few small parts to be replaced."

"That is about it."

"Couldn't I—" Bob began but Mr. Crowninshield held up a cautioning finger.

"I'd rather have you on shore," announced he quietly. Then turning to the electricians he added, "I suppose the radio aboard the yacht does not differ much from this set. There will be nothing but what you can handle."

"Nothing, sir; nothing at all," was the answer. "Besides, we are quite familiar with shipboard equipment. We do a lot of such work. Just before we came down here we went down to Long Island and put the *Siren*, a very fine steam yacht, into shape."

"The *Siren*, eh?" repeated Mr. Crowninshield as indifferently as he could.

"Yes, sir. Perhaps you know the boat, sir."

"I've never been aboard her," replied the capitalist slowly. "She belongs to——"

"To Mr. Daly, sir. As fine a yacht as was ever in the water."

Daly! At the name both Bob and his employer started. It was the very man Mr. Crowninshield had suspected.

"So Daly has a place down on Long Island, has he?" drawled he.

"Oh, no, sir. Mr. Daly's place is on an island off the Maine coast. He had just put in at the Long Island port for some minor repairs. He said he was going to cruise a while this summer and wanted to be sure everything was shipshape before going to Maine. The mate told me they were waiting to pick up some people at Buzzard's Bay."

"Going to take the yacht through the Canal?"

"Yes."

"An interesting trip," observed Mr. Crowninshield slowly.

"That Canal is quite a time saver for New Yorkers." He yawned and started to move away. Bob held his breath, waiting.

"I suppose you don't know where Daly was going for his cruise," inquired he over his shoulder.

"No, sir, I don't," was the response of the workman who seemed flattered at having aroused this degree of interest in his story. "I believe, though, that before they started they were to put into Newport for provisions."

Newport! Then it was doubtless Newport where O'Connel was to be taken aboard! Bob dared not raise his eyes lest the excitement that danced in them be detected.

"And after provisioning up there Daly was to cruise, eh?" called Mr. Crowninshield. "Well, the Atlantic is wide and he will have plenty of room."

"That's right, sir," chuckled the mechanic, delighted by the condescension of the great man whom all New Yorkers knew by reputation. Think of hobnobbing in this pleasant fashion with one of the big financiers of Wall Street!

"How simple and kind a gentleman Mr. Crowninshield is!" commented he patronizingly after the capitalist was out of hearing. "And so artless!"

Bob struggled not to smile.

Kind Mr. Crowninshield might be but hardly simple. Certainly not artless. What a rare lot of amusing incidents the world contained!

CHAPTER XIV

BOB AS PEDAGOGUE

The wireless was now in commission and the next morning, after having waited until the hour designated for O'Connel's signal and received no message, Bob and his pupils assembled for their first lesson, not in a stuffy room but on the broad, well-shaded veranda of Surfside. A cool breeze rippled the water, stirring it into tiny waves and as Dick dropped into one of the big wicker chairs he fidgeted to be out in the freshly-painted knockabout that bobbed invitingly at the float.

His father intercepted his yearning glance and instantly interpreted it.

"Come, now!" said he half playfully. "Quit making sheep's eyes at that boat, son. An hour's wireless lesson isn't going to cut your morning very short or prevent you from having plenty of time to sail, swim, or motor. Whether it does or not you've got to endure it. Your summer holiday is long enough in all conscience. If I had until October with nothing more arduous to do than put up with an hour's instruction early each day I should think myself almighty lucky."

"I am lucky, Dad," conceded Dick quickly, "only——"

"Lucky! I should say you were! You don't know what work means. Well, it was you who wanted this radio outfit. You were all for it and——"

"I am for it still, Dad," interrupted Dick eagerly.

"Then go to it and master it," retorted his father. "If you do not relish the lessons, swallow them down for the sake of the fun you are going to have later; for if you are intelligent enough to handle your wireless with some brain and understanding you are going to enjoy it a hundred percent more in the end."

"I know I shall," Dick agreed. "It is only that I am crazy to get at the thing itself."

The boy's father shook his head.

"You are like all your generation," said he severely. "Eager to leap the preliminaries and land at the top of the ladder with the first bound. It is an impatient age and the vice extends to the old as well as the young. Nobody wants to fit himself for anything nowadays. In my youth men expected to serve apprenticeships and did not hope to achieve a position until they had learned how to fill it. But now everybody leaps at the big job and the big salary that goes with it and blunders along, taking out his ignorance and lack of experience on the general public. As for you youngsters, you covet at fifteen everything that those who are fifty have. You want automobiles, boats, victrolas and radio telephones before you know how to run them, much less pay for them. Look at Bob, here. He is worth two of you for he can earn what he has. Often I tell myself I am a fool to indulge you and Nancy as I do. I ought by rights to make you do without what you want until you can foot the bill for it." Mr. Crowninshield took a few hasty paces across the piazza. "Still," added he, his voice softening, "I fancy that scheme would be a sight harder on me than on you, for I like nothing better than to get you what you want."

For a moment he paused, looking fondly at his son. Then as if afraid of himself he bristled and continued: "But to return to this wireless—remember that if you do not learn something about it and how to use it I shall take it away. I mean it, mind!"

"Yes, Dad," was the timid answer.

With this awful alternative looming like a specter in his path was it to be wondered at that Dick resolutely turned his gaze from the allurements of the harbor and settled himself in the big chair with all his attention focussed on Bob King's radio lesson. Moreover, human nature is selfish enough to like company in its misery and were not his mother, Nancy and Walter consigned to the same fate as himself?

Therefore the initial lesson began gayly.

At first Bob, seated in the chair of state facing his class, was shy and embarrassed; but soon he forgot himself in his subject and losing his hesitancy he spoke with the authority of one who has mastered his art.

"I am going to begin," said he, "just as they began with me at the radio station, for I think if you get the principles of wireless at the outset you will find it much easier to understand it. And to do this we shall not start with wires, generators, detectors, or anything of that sort; instead we must go back of them all to the earth and the air, and learn how it is possible for sound to travel without the aid of human devices. For in reality there is something that takes the place of man-made wires. This is the ether. Surrounding the earth moves the air we breathe; and as we go higher this air becomes thinner and thinner until, by and by, a height is reached where the air gives place to ether, a sort of radiant energy that bridges the zone between the air space that encircles the earth and the sun, and brings to us its heat. This great sea of ether is made up of particles that are never still and which are so small that they get between every substance they encounter, thereby becoming a universal medium for transmitting light, heat, color and many other things to our earth. Without this body of ether, there would be no agency to pass on to us (as well as to the many other planets of our solar system and those outside it) the energy the sun generates, which is the thing that keeps us alive."

Bob waited a moment to make sure that his point was clear and then proceeded:

"Now this energy as it moves through the ether takes the form of waves; and these waves go out not in a single train but since the ether is continually disturbed by the sun, in series of wave trains that vary in frequency. Such waves are electromagnetic in character, and light, heat, sound, and the waves carrying wireless messages are all of a similar type, differing only in their relative rates of vibration. If unobstructed, and moving through free ether, all of them travel at practically the same velocity, that is about one hundred eighty-six thousand miles a second. When, however, they encounter other substances, as they are continually bound to do, this rate of velocity changes. The waves of sound, for example, sent out by the wireless telephone are very slow compared with the high-rate vibrations that produce waves resulting in light."

Again the youthful teacher paused.

"Now this constant turmoil in the ether which creates the magnetic area explains why the magnetized needle of a compass unfailingly points north and south. This one simple fact is a certain proof of its existence. And once granting a magnetic field to be there it is less difficult to understand how wireless waves are produced in this congenial medium and find their way through it, following in their journey the curve of the earth's surface."

Bob smiled at his audience encouragingly.

"If you can once get this wave law through your heads the

rest is not hard," asserted he, "for the whole wireless system is based on wave motion."

"With an ocean spread out before us we ought to be able to understand waves," interpolated Nancy.

"We ought," nodded Bob. "And yet better than using the ocean as an illustration imagine a small pond. Think, instead, of a nice quiet little round pond if you can. Now when you chuck a stick or a pebble into that still water you know how the ripples will at once go out. There will be rings of them, and the bigger they get the fainter they will be. In other words, as the area widens the strength of the waves decreases; and as this same principle applies to radio you can see that it takes a lot of energy from a wireless station to reach a receiver a great distance away."

"I've got that!" cried Dick with such spontaneity that every one laughed.

"Wave lengths, however, have nothing to do with actual distance," went on Bob quickly. "Of course we think of the wave length as the distance between one ridge of water and another. There is, though, no law that would make it possible to translate these spaces into our scale of miles, for sometimes they are near together, sometimes far apart. Distance, therefore, depends on the speed with which the wave travels and the frequency with which the water is disturbed. If you keep tossing things in quick succession into the water you will get a correspondingly quick succession of waves. The law governing wireless waves is exactly the same. Their length depends on the velocity of the wave and the frequency of the oscillations that cause it. Or to put it another way, in order to reckon a wave length you must determine its velocity (which is not impossible when you remember that sound travels about one thousand one hundred and twenty feet every second) and the number of vibrations the particular note causing the wave is making per second. Now science has been able to compute just how many complete vibrations a certain note, key, or pitch as you may please to call it, makes each second, or how many times the particles of air vibrate back and forth when that especial note is sent out.

"Suppose, for example, a note makes 240 complete vibrations a second while traveling 1,120 feet; if we divide 1,120 by 240 we shall get 4.66 as the wave length of this note. So it is the pitch to which a note is keyed that helps determine its distance; and the force employed to start the note sent out through the magnetic field. That is why a message projected into the ether from a high-power station carries a greater distance than one sent from a station where the power is weaker. It is by power and pitch, then, not by length that we gauge wireless waves. Do you see that?"

A chorus of assent greeted the question.

"That's bully!" Bob announced boyishly; then blushed at the undignified ejaculation.

"Don't you be fussed, young man," smiled Mr. Crowninshield. "We're all of an age here."

"I quite forgot," apologized the tutor.

"That is exactly what I want you to do," returned the master of Surfside. "Ignore us old people. We are only listening in, anyway, and have no earthly right to be here."

"Still, I wish to treat you with——"

"It's all right, Bob. We understand," put in Mrs. Crowninshield reassuringly.

"Well, then, if you will excuse me I'm off again," replied the boy. "And now that we've got wave lengths settled to our satisfaction we must remember some other things. One is that sound travels not only through the air but through the water. In fact, sounds are louder under water than they are above it. Water is not only a better medium for carrying sound but also, since it contains fewer obstructions, sound waves travel farther through it. Another thing which we must not forget is that our ears do not hear all the sounds that go on about us. The merciful Lord has arranged that when there are less than twenty-four vibrations a second, or more than forty thousand they escape us. But a wireless instrument, on the contrary is spared nothing, having attached to it a detector that catches every sound and an amplifier that magnifies it and makes it discernible to our ears. When you listen in on a wireless telephone you will be uncontestably conscious of this. Also you must take into consideration that the waves sent out by a radio transmitter are not choppy, irregular ones such as you get when a stone is tossed into the water; wireless waves go out in regular, well-formed relays that neither overlap nor obscure one another. Were this not so the signals made would be jumbled together and utterly unintelligible."

"Sure they would!" Bob's young brother nodded.

"Now to insure these several results we are compelled to resort to the help of scientific apparatus. Therefore at every receiving station we have devices that will intercept the waves as they come in; retransform them into electrical oscillations; and catching the weak oscillations make them strong enough to be read. Hence we use some type of induction coil by means of which a battery current of such low pressure and diffused flow as scarcely to be felt will be transformed or concentrated into a pressure that is very powerful. In order to form wireless waves we must have a frequency of at least one hundred thousand vibrations a second; and as it is out of the question to produce these by mechanical means we employ a group of Leyden jars. Such jars you have of course seen. They have in them two pieces of tinfoil separated by glass, which is a nonconductor of electric currents, and various other acids and minerals. When you connect a number of these small jars together you have a battery as powerful as that of a large single jar."

"I never saw jars like those," objected Dick.

Bob beamed at the intelligence of the demurrer.

"When I say jar," explained he, "it does not necessarily mean that these jars are of the round, cylindrical shape that comes to mind when you mention the word; on the contrary Leyden jars are often flat because such a form makes them more compact. That is also why we use several little ones instead of one big one. But whatever their shape the principle involved is always the same. When the terminals are connected with a current, the jar will not only receive but will retain a charge equal in pressure to that of the device sending the current. And when you go even farther and bring the terminals near together, the quick discharge that takes place creates an electric spark which is in reality a series of alternating flashes that come so fast as to be blurred into what appears to be one. Could we separate these flashes we should find that each of them lasts less than a thousandth part of a second. The frequency of such oscillations is regulated by what is technically termed capacity, that is the size of the Leyden jar. The smaller the capacity the greater the frequency of the flashes.

"Now this spark, or oscillatory discharge emitted from the Leyden jar, does not result from a single traveling of the current all in one direction; instead the electricity moves back and forth, or alternates, and the space where the discharge takes place (and which, by the way, can be lengthened or decreased as pleases the operator) is known as the spark gap."

"But I should think this explosion of the spark would make a noise," commented Walter.

"Bully for you, little brother!" returned Bob, smiling at His Highness. "You are quite an electrician. If the current is strong, or, in other words, if the discharge is a high frequency one, it does. Hence something has to be used to deaden the sound just as a muffler is used on a motor boat. It is important, however, that this muffler should not prevent the operator from watching the condition of his spark for otherwise he could not keep track of his battery or know whether it was on the job or not. So you will find little peepholes of mica or glass in the sides of the muffler."

"Windows," murmured Nancy grasping the idea and translating it into the vernacular.

"Exactly," Bob agreed. Evidently his audience were understanding what he was trying to make clear to them.

"Now we have our high frequency oscillations occurring in the spark discharged from the Leyden jar and jumping the spark gap; nevertheless they would not do us any good were there not some way to use and regulate them. This brings us to the induction coil of which I spoke a second ago."

"It sounds very terrible," smiled Mrs. Crowninshield.

"It isn't, though," answered Bob, returning the smile. "In fact it is a very simple device—nothing more than a dozen or so twists of copper wire reeled about a wooden frame exactly as strands of thread might be wound round a spool. One end of the inductance is connected permanently with the ground and from the other end two movable wires go out, one of which can be connected with the spark gap and the other with the antenna that goes into the air and catches the sound waves. There isn't anything very terrible about that, you see."

"Antenna is what butterflies have," suggested Nancy vaguely.

"Quite right!" assented the wireless man. "Only radio antennæ are not to feel with—at least not in the same way. Nevertheless they do reach out and capture the sound. On all wireless stations you will notice the masts that support them. Sometimes there is one wire, sometimes a group. It is the wires themselves, remember, not the masts, which are the antennæ. Nowadays, however, you will occasionally see an indoor aerial used in connection with small, low-power outfits. It does away with the masts and outside equipment and frequently serves the same purpose quite satisfactorily. But most persons prefer the older method and for long-distance work it has, up to date proved to be indispensable. Now the antenna has both electrical capacity and inductance, and when connected up with the apparatus a wireless operator can at will cause it to disturb the magnetic fields surrounding the earth."

"You didn't say how high these masts had to be, Bob," put in Mr. Crowninshield. "Are they always the same length?"

"Oh, no, indeed, sir," was the prompt response. "Their length varies according to the type of service required of them. I'm glad you asked the question. Sometimes the masts are about two hundred feet high; again they may approximate four hundred and eighteen feet. And sometimes in emergencies you will discover no masts at all, the wires being fastened instead to captive balloons or kites which hold them in place long enough to send or receive hasty messages. This latter method is usually resorted to in wartime or during army or navy maneuvers. There are also compact radio sets to be had that can be carried on muleback and set up and taken down on a hurried army march. On shipboard the ordinary masts of the vessel serve, of course, to support the antenna."

"Thank you, Bob. That is exactly what I wanted to know," said Mr. Crowninshield.

"I'm glad, sir. Now you'd think by this time we had everything necessary to produce our wireless waves and yet we haven't. There is still one thing almost more important than all the rest that we have not yet spoken of."

"What's that, Bob?" piped Walter.

"The tuner. You recall that at the beginning I mentioned the pitch, note, or key of the sound produced or received?"

"Yes," returned the class in chorus.

"Well, it is in that tune or pitch, or whatever you prefer to call it, that a large measure of the secret of wireless lies. To be successful in getting and sending messages we must tune the oscillations, or key the signals caused by the discharge of the battery in our Leyden jar, so that they will be in harmony (or at precisely the same pitch) with the antenna circuit. That is, the parts of the instrument must synchronize, just as two persons who would talk together must speak in the same language. This adjustment is made in the inductance coil because although both the Leyden jar where the spark is generated that causes the oscillations and the antenna can be regulated independently of each other, a few turns of the inductance coil affects each circuit. After the two circuits have been adjusted to the same frequency they are said to synchronize. Often to reach this result a device is used that states precisely the wave length, and after the frequency of one circuit has been ascertained the other can easily be adjusted to correspond with it. The length of the wave is, you see, dependent on the largeness of the antenna and the capacity, or strength of current, of the Leyden jar. Just as a child uses a big stone to produce the largest splash and greatest waves so we must have a powerful force behind our wave lengths to make them carry most successfully. In accordance with this law, generally speaking, we find short wave lengths used for low power, short-distance outfits; and long wave lengths for high-power circuits whose aim is to traverse continents and oceans."

Bob pushed back his chair.

"I think," said he, "we have now come to a good stopping place and we will call the lesson off for to-day. If you digest all I have told you, you will have had an ample radio starter."

"You haven't said much about sending messages," complained Dick.

"That is quite another story," smiled the boy's tutor, "and such a long one that were I to tell it to you now it would mean you would get no sailing or swimming to-day."

Instantly Dick was on his feet, Leyden jars and inductance coils forgotten.

"We'll cut it out then," he laughed. "Who is for a swim? I'll race any man to the bath-house!" And off he went at top speed.

CHAPTER XV

TIDINGS

Two days later O'Connel's first signal came.

Bob was at his early morning task of oiling and tightening up his apparatus and cleaning it, and both Dick and Walter were hovering near, watching him and learning all they could concerning the proper care of the equipment. Having made everything shipshape the young radio operator slipped the double head receiver over his forehead and prepared to listen in for his customary interval. Suddenly the boys saw him start excitedly and motion them to stop talking. With face alight he was leaning forward eagerly. Then came the sharp click of the Morse code and after an interval with radiant face the elder lad wriggled out of his trappings.

"What is it? What is it?" cried his two companions, hardly able to contain their curiosity.

"It was O'Connel."

"What did he say? Is the dog there? Where was the yacht?" Breathlessly the questions tumbled one over the other.

"The *Siren* is anchored off Gloucester and bound north, probably to Bar Harbor. A dog they call Trixie, but which O'Connel thinks is Lola, is aboard the boat. The description we gave him seems to fit her. He says she isn't very well—won't eat and seems either homesick or seasick. Mr. Daly is quite worried about her."

"For goodness' sake don't tell Dad or Mother that. They'll have a fit," Dick cried. "Should Lola die I believe my father would shoot Daly down."

"But I've got to give him the message."

"You needn't repeat all of it, need you?"

"Oh, I think you ought to tell them," Walter put in. "They would rather know, I'm sure."

"Dad will storm fit to raise the dead."

"We can't help it," answered His Highness.

"I am of the kid's opinion," Bob replied slowly. "I think we should tell your father and mother the whole truth just as O'Connel has sent it."

"Prepare for a nice, pleasant tornado, then," said Dick, "for you will get it all right."

"I wish I could have talked with O'Connel," declared Bob thoughtfully. "I did all I dared. You see, until our license comes I am not expected to transmit messages from this station. We have to get from the government both an operator's license and a permit for the station; and although I put in the application promptly there is so much red tape about it that it seems as if the inspector would never show up. If I had been caught sending a message this morning without these blooming papers there would have been the deuce of a row. However, I took a chance because I felt the emergency demanded it, and because being one of Uncle Sam's own men he couldn't very well put up the kick that I was not competent to handle a wireless outfit. Still, I shan't dare do it again."

"Isn't there anything we can do to hustle up the inspector?" inquired Dick.

"I'm afraid not, son. Government inspectors are not a hurrying race," was Bob's whimsical reply. "However, I telephoned our local man yesterday and something may happen to-day. He and I used to be on quite good terms when he occasionally dropped in at Seaver Bay. I told him that if I could not get a station license pretty soon our whole outfit would be no good to us this season. He promised he would take up the matter at once. With that I had to be satisfied. Whether he does anything or not remains to be seen."

"I suppose O'Connel understands this difficulty, doesn't he?" mused Dick.

"Oh, he knows, all right, why I can't answer him. I've assured him that his tidings have come through and that is all he wants to know," Bob answered. "He has dealt with the government himself and is familiar with its deliberate habits. Besides, there really isn't much we can say."

"Maybe you think that," grinned Dick, "but wait until you tell Dad that Lola is sick and hear him sputter. You will believe then that there is quite a bit that can be said. And if you get my mother to add her comments you will have plenty to relay over the wire."

The prophecy was indeed true, as Bob King proved after he had raced across the grass and overtaken Mr. and Mrs. Crowninshield on a tour of inspection to the rose gardens.

"News, Bob?" questioned the capitalist, wheeling about to meet the flying figure. "What is it? Let us have it quickly."

Carefully the message was repeated.

"Off Gloucester, eh, and bound north? Humph! And they've re-christened the poor little pupsie Trixie! Hang them! O'Connel thinks she isn't well? Of course she isn't seasick. Lola has been out on our yacht a hundred times. The reason she won't eat is because she is lonesome—misses her home and family. The wretches! I wish I had Daly here! I'd wring his neck," blustered Mr. Crowninshield.

"Isn't there anything we can do, Archibald? We simply must get that dog back before she dies. Poor little Lola! She was such a dependent little creature. It is terrible, terrible!"

"There, there, my dear! Don't go all to pieces over it. Aren't we doing all we can? Do you want Daly to smell a rat and toss his stolen property into the sea? Dacie says to give him rope enough and in time he will hang himself, and I am inclined to think the advice wise. Still, that does not prevent me from wishing I could lay hands on Daly. I'd like nothing better than to thrash the life out of him."

"I suppose you will telephone the detective the news we've received," suggested Bob, in order to quell the rising storm and divert Mr. Crowninshield's attention.

"Yes, I'll get New York on the wire right away. It is as well Lyman and his pal should know Lola is sick and that they can't dally round forever."

"Shall you be back for the wireless lesson?" called Bob, uncertain whether to ask the question or not.

"Oh, sure! It won't help matters for us to sit around and wail the whole morning. We'll be on deck for your radio talk at the usual time."

"All right, sir."

True to their agreement, at the appointed hour both Mr. and Mrs. Crowninshield made their appearance on the piazza and joined the group of young people who awaited their coming. They had, as Bob expressed it, cooled off a bit and were no longer in such an agitated frame of mind; nevertheless anxiety had left its mark by keying the master's voice to a sharper note, and shadowing the lady's brow with a frown of annoyance.

"I suppose you let out on O'Connel, didn't you, after he got through talking this morning?" was the first remark of the owner of Surfside.

"I couldn't say more than a word. Our license hasn't come yet, you know."

"That's so, darn it! I never saw anything in all my born life with so many rules attached to it as this wireless business. It is one tangle of rules, rules, rules! You might as well be tied up in a net," fretted the man.

"There do seem to be a good many rules at first glance," returned Bob pleasantly. "However, when you examine them most of them are both necessary and wise. And after all when each radio operator knows in black and white what he can do and what he can't it is far simpler."

"I suppose so," grumbled Mr. Crowninshield.

"Besides, there are always slackers at every job," continued Bob. "Rules help to keep such persons up to the mark and prevent carelessness and accidents."

"Yes, I fancy that is so," came more graciously from the still irate gentleman.

"Then all stations are not alike. That compass station at Bell Reef, for example, that you were asking me about yesterday; the government lays out specific duties and makes special rules for such a station, as in fact it does for all radio stations. Some of these rules relate to the care of the place and the cleaning and general overhauling of apparatus at stated intervals. There are, you see, certain instruments which must be cleaned and readjusted every day; certain others every week, others every month, and some every six months. It simply means making sure that your outfit is in the pink of condition with every part functioning as it should. There are, of course, operators who would see that this was done anyway, rules or no rules; but like every other profession there might be men who, off on an isolated spot with no one to keep them up to the mark, would grow careless and slovenly. Too much depends on wireless stations to run the risk of errors through imperfections in the equipment."

"I can understand all that; but aren't there a score of other regulations?"

"You mean about what they shall and shall not do?"

"Yes."

"There certainly are. There have to be because we have several different types of land stations. Just as the shipboard stations have their special kinds of work, so do those on shore. For example, there are two different classes of radio compass stations,—those that operate independently and are located with a view to giving good cross-bearings to vessels that are from fifty to a hundred miles out to sea; and those known as harbor stations which are governed by a central control station and designed to inform ships within thirty miles of the entrance to outer channels of their position. The function of each of these stations is, as you can see, quite different and therefore each of them is obliged to have its own set of rules."

"I never knew anything about radio compass stations before," announced Dick.

"That is because you never sailed the seas and had to call on one for aid," smiled Bob. "If you did you would be very thankful, I guess, that the government has so carefully provided some one to answer just the sort of question you wished answered. I try to remember this when I get hot under the collar because the license for our station does not arrive. Uncle Sam can't help it if his men are slow. The plan at the top is all right. There must be rules to govern wireless stations, be they governmental, commercial, or private; rules to regulate the wave lengths each may use; rules to make sure the operators who have charge of them know their job; and inspectors to make sure that every such rule is obeyed."

"Who has the big chore of following up all these people and making certain that they are conforming to the law?" questioned Mr. Crowninshield.

"The Department of Commerce issues the licenses for all private and commercial stations and sends its inspectors to keep an eye on whatever comes under their control. It is this department that will have jurisdiction over Surfside if the license is granted. Government radio stations on the other hand, not only the high-power class but the coastal stations and everything that pertains to their relations with commercial stations afloat or ashore, whether in the United States or in foreign lands are entirely under the control of the Director of Naval Communications of the Navy Department."

"I wish you'd tell us something more about compass stations," Dick said. "Were you ever stationed at one?"

"Yes, for a little while I was on an island off the coast," replied Bob. "But I did not like it very well and applied for a transfer."

"It must have been lonely as the dickens on an island; worse, even, than being at Seaver Bay. Why in goodness did they build the station there?"

"Why, you see, a compass station that operates independently as that one did is usually situated on a lightship or an island because that location is best suited to the sort of work it has to do."

"And that is?"

"To give ships their positions when they sing out to ask exactly where they are," replied Bob. "Since the station is fairly well out to sea itself, it is able to furnish excellent cross-bearings and set the vessel on her course in case she is off it. Ships have been known to miss their way, you know, especially in a fog; and if they have not missed it they are often very grateful to be assured they have not and that their own calculations were correct. So the rule is that an operator must always be listening in for at least three minutes at ten, twenty-five, forty, and fifty-five minutes past the hour and be ready to answer a Q T E when he hears it."

"What's a Q T E?" inquired both Dick and Walter simultaneously.

"Those particular letters mean: *What is my true bearing?* It takes less time to send the letters than to spell out the entire sentence and therefore a simple code which means the same in all languages is used. When such a call is received the operator replies: Q T S (meaning: Your true bearing is) and then follows it with the number of degrees from his radio post stated in words, and also the name of the station responding to the message. It is a general rule, by-the-by, that all numerals used in any wireless communication must be spelled out to make sure of their being perfectly understood."

"What a bother!" ejaculated Walter.

"It prevents mistakes, brother; and if it does that it is certainly worth the trouble."

"I suppose so," answered His Highness a trifle crestfallen.

"Then what do you say next?" interrupted Dick, who was much interested in the subject in hand.

"Well, after you have given the true bearing the ship wires: Q T F."

"And that means?"

"*What is my position?*"

"And you have to repeat those words before giving it just as you did before?" asked Dick.

"Always," nodded Bob. "Every question asked is always repeated by the operator answering it to make sure that each party fully understands what is being talked about. You can't risk having a ship complain: 'Oh, I thought those figures you sent me were so-and-so.' No, indeed. Everything must be so explicit that there will be no room for blunders. So after you have repeated the question you send the latitude and longitude *in words.*"

"I guess there is sense in the rules after all," smiled Mrs. Crowninshield. "Thus far we have not discovered any which, on being examined, were not both reasonable and wise."

"That's the way I feel," Bob rejoined. "After being in radio work and seeing the opportunities there are for mistakes, I have decided operators cannot be too careful. You see it is not like talking with a person face to face. Those you are communicating with are usually miles and miles away. Such stations as I have been telling you about are on the lookout for any six-hundred-meter calls and they answer in this tune. After communication with a ship is established, however, the tune shifts to seven hundred and fifty-six meters if a Navy vessel should be talking; if not, the six-hundred-meter wave length assigned is used. This leaves the shorter range waves to commercial vessels and greatly simplifies matters."

"That is a good rule, too," chimed in Mr. Crowninshield.

"And now about the harbor stations," suggested Dick.

The young tutor smiled.

"I had not intended to give you all this stuff this morning," protested he, "but since you are interested in it we may as well go on with the subject. The task of the harbor stations, then, is to listen both on a six-hundred-meter range, and one of nine hundred and fifty-two—the first wave length for commercial and the latter for Navy ship's calls. Then in response to inquiry the operator directs the vessel how to enter that particular harbor, stating just where the entrance buoys are and where the channel lies. If the man at the wheel is new to the port this aid is invaluable."

"Not much like the navigation of the old days, is it?" mused Mr. Crowninshield. "I should think such stations would put pilots out of business."

"They do to some extent," was the reply. "There are, however, always ships that cannot make a landing under their own steam, ships that have to be towed. So the pilots still find something to do."

"And are these harbor stations on islands too?" questioned Nancy.

"Many of them are. A small proportion of them, though, are in lighthouses. It all depends on which place has the more favorable location."

"But do not the land stations that send messages sometimes interfere with these stations?" queried Mr. Crowninshield.

"There are rules to prevent *that*," laughed Bob. "Of course the difference in wave length to which the various types of stations are limited solves a part of this difficulty. As I told you commercial stations have their own particular wave length and must stick to it; and private stations such as this one here have their range of two hundred meters in which to operate and are confined to not more than one kilowatt for sending messages. You cannot use more than this without special permission from the Secretary of Labor. Should you do so you are liable to a fine of one hundred dollars if your offense is deliberate; if, however, it is proved that your apparatus was out of adjustment and overreached itself you may get off with a twenty-five-dollar fine. In that case you must see at once that your radio error is corrected and your outfit set right."

"But sometimes along the coast aren't there big government stations belonging to the army or navy? I should think these, with their press of business, would butt in on the smaller ones and raise havoc with them," ventured Mr. Crowninshield.

"Where there are such mix-ups and private or commercial stations interfere with important government outfits the smaller ones are not allowed to send messages during the first fifteen minutes of each hour, such time being reserved for government business. The government, on the other hand, must respect the rights of the littler chap and use this particular interval for transmitting. In fact, when licenses are issued this condition is made with private owners and the station is so listed. Of course, however, should an S O S call come, all rules go by the boards and the distress call has the right of way in every case."

Mrs. Crowninshield, smiling mischievously, rose from her chair.

"There is an S O S coming in right now for a lemonade," said she, fanning herself with her filmy handkerchief. "Who will join me?"

A chorus of "I!" "I!" greeted the question.

She touched a bell.

"Bring lemonade for six, Emelie," said she. "Put in some slices of orange, some strawberries, and plenty of cracked ice. What a warm day it is! I am glad I am not out on some hot, sun-baked island answering radio calls."

"You probably would not be hot if you were on an island out to sea, my dear," her husband returned playfully. "However, I'll agree that this veranda is good enough for me on a July day."

The tinkling of ice cut short the conversation. Far away through the house its distant cadence sounded.

"The first and tallest lemonade must be for Bob," Nancy announced. "He has certainly earned it."

CHAPTER XVI

MIRACLES

Although throughout the day Mr. Crowninshield did not wander far from the telephone no word came from the New York detectives and evening saw him quite discouraged.

"I cannot imagine what those fellows are up to," fretted he. "Now that they know where the yacht is and have had all day to do something about it, it is beyond my comprehension why they haven't. Lola will be dead before they get round to moving on Daly."

"I don't believe they are sitting idle," Bob declared in an effort to cheer his patron. "Probably there will be news to-morrow."

"Maybe," sighed the financier. "But if something does not happen by to-morrow, I shall start myself in my own yacht to chase up Daly."

"I doubt if that would do any good, sir," protested Bob. "It might simply, as you said yourself, precipitate a crisis."

"Well, a crisis is better than having nothing done," fumed the man irritably.

"You must not forget there is O'Connel."

"Much good he is doing. We have only heard from him once and as we have no license you can't talk to him."

"Nevertheless, he is on the job at his end of the line," Bob answered. "He has a lot of common sense, too. You can trust him to keep tabs on how things are moving."

"Maybe I can. I hope so," was the dismal retort.

Evening, however, saw no improvement in Mr. Crowninshield's mood. "Not a yip of any sort from those chaps in New York. One would think they were dead," he growled. "Well, I'll give them one more day and then if they haven't something to show I will send them to blazes and take up the case myself. I almost wish I had done it in the first place. Here I am paying a small fortune and getting no results."

Again Bob struggled to soothe the perturbed mind and raise the capitalist's spirits.

"Oh, we'll hear something to-morrow, I guess," said he with an optimism he did not altogether feel. "Maybe my license will come; or the inspector may appear; or O'Connel may send tidings; or news may come from New York. Something is sure to happen. Why don't we all go over to the station and listen in on the broadcasting to-night. We are sure to get something that will be interesting and now that the 'loud speaker' is in position we shall be able to hear without using individual receivers. You haven't any of you really heard what our wireless can do."

"I know it," acknowledged the gentleman. "You see, just about every night during broadcasting hours we have either had company or I have been busy."

"But are you to be busy to-night?" inquired Bob.

"No, I fancy we're not. Mrs. Crowninshield said there was nothing on."

"Then why don't we light up the boathouse, and all of us listen to what is going on in the world," Bob suggested. "I wish, too, Jerry might come. He has not had a chance to see the outfit at all, much less hear it. If it would not annoy you and the ladies just to let him sit at the back of the room he could hear everything now that the horn is on." Bob hesitated. "He has been so kind about helping us——"

"Sure! Ask him by all means," Mr. Crowninshield assented heartily. "Or better yet, I will ask him myself. I am glad you reminded me of it. Jerry is my right-hand man and I like to give him pleasure when I can. What time will your show begin?"

"Oh, from seven o'clock on there is usually something doing, sir. But the most interesting part of the program begins at eight."

"We'll be on hand, then."

This promise won, Bob imparted the tidings to Dick and Walter and the two assistants, as they dubbed themselves, hastened to prepare the new radio building for the reception of guests. Comfortable chairs and gay cushions were brought from the house and in his enthusiasm Dick even went so far as to drape a flag over the entrance of the low room.

"We might have hung out bunting if we'd known sooner they were coming," said he.

"I guess they won't care about the bunting once they are inside the place," Walter asserted in a comforting tone.

"Don't you hope the outfit will show up well? I do," declared Dick. "It would be just our luck to have something act up so we couldn't hear anything. Then Dad, who is feeling pretty much on edge anyway, would announce that a wireless was simply money thrown in a hole."

"We're not responsible for the conditions," laughed Bob. "If static is bothersome it is not our fault."

"Nevertheless, Dad wouldn't understand that. He would just think we did not know how to operate the thing."

"Well, we'll pray for moderate quiet," smiled Bob. "Of course I'd like the apparatus to show off at its best. But like a child, it probably won't. We shall have to take our luck; and if we do not get satisfactory results to-night why the audience will have to come again to-morrow or some other time."

"Maybe it won't—at least maybe Dad won't," Dick answered incoherently. "If he starts off in the yacht to-morrow———"

"Oh, he won't set off to chase Daly to-morrow, don't you fret," put in His Highness. "He was only sputtering. What good could he do? He wouldn't have any right to search the *Siren* even if he overtook her; nor could he arrest the criminals aboard her. Daly would pitch Lola over the side of the boat before he would stand by and let your father board his yacht and he knows it."

"Maybe he does," admitted Dick. "Still, he was tremendously in earnest this afternoon."

"He has calmed down some now," His Highness replied.

"I hope he'll stay calmed," Dick smiled. "Perhaps, unless our show goes wrong and he gets irate at the radio company, he will."

In fact had the three young wireless operators been willing to admit it they were far more perturbed when they heard the invited company approaching than they would have been willing to confess. In the heart of each of them was the same thought: the new radiophone must justify itself and prove that it was worth all the money that had been expended upon it.

"Well, here we are! And here's Jerry, too. He said he couldn't possibly come—tried to make me believe he was too busy, the rascal. But I labored with him and finally got him here," announced the master triumphantly.

Very hot and very uncomfortable under the general banter Jerry blushed.

"Now where do you wish to put us, Dick?" inquired the boy's mother. "We are under your orders to-night—yours and Bob's."

"I think you will be able to hear in any of these chairs—that is, if we hear at all," Dick responded nervously.

"What do you mean by *able to hear at all?*" put in his father sharply.

"Why—eh—sometimes conditions vary," was the ambiguous answer. "One does not always hear equally well." It seemed wiser to prepare his father's mind for possible disappointment.

In the meantime Bob was tinkering with the plugs.

"Everybody ready?" he asked.

"All on deck!" came from Mr. Crowninshield whose depression, it was plain to be seen, had momentarily vanished.

"Then here goes!" cried Bob.

Instantly the quiet of the room was transformed into a chaos of sound. There was a shrill piping as of a singing wind, and a wail that echoed hauntingly through the air as the tuner revolved.

"What in the name of goodness——?" began Mr. Crowninshield.

"Hush, Dad! It is always like that," explained Dick hastily.

"But it's horrible."

"Yes, I know. But wait."

"Isn't something out of order?"

"No." Dick smiled patronizingly.

"My soul and body," whispered Jerry from his corner, "did anybody ever hear such a sound? Ain't it the wind outside. Seems as if a gale must have come up—a hurricane, tornado, or something. If a storm's coming I can't sit round here. I'll have to be seeing to the awnings or they'll be ripped to pieces." He half rose from his chair.

"Don't worry, Jerry; everything's all right outside," interrupted Walter reassuringly.

"You mean to say it's just in here?" murmured the bewildered Jerry. Enjoying the old man's confusion, Walter nodded.

"What you hear is the rise of our pitch," explained Dick.

"I should think it was the rise of something," grumbled Mr. Crowninshield.

"We are running up our meters in order to catch the higher tuned waves," Bob added. "That is part of the bedlam."

"And the rest?"

"It is static interference."

"What's that?"

"Well, static is the big bugbear of radio," answered Bob, pausing a moment in regulating his tuner and detector. "It is caused by stray waves moving in various directions through the atmosphere, and by electrical conditions. It is the defect all wireless people have to fight. Sometimes it is worse than others and unfortunately to-night it promises to be pretty bad. You see it has been a close, heavy day and no doubt thunderstorms are in the air. A thunderstorm will kick up no end of a rumpus with wireless."

"But we haven't had any thunderstorm," Nancy called above the hubbub.

"No, but somebody else's thunderstorm would bother us almost as much," Bob explained good-humoredly.

"Never mind the thunderstorms now," put in Mr. Crowninshield. "Aren't we going to hear anything but this whistling and groaning? Whee! There it goes again. It is for all the world like a chorus of cats."

"It is more like a siren horn tooting up and down," laughed Nancy.

A spluttering crackle blotted out the wail.

"You would think they were frying doughnuts," grinned Dick, "wouldn't you?"

"And you really believe a thunderstorm would cause a noise like this?" queried Mrs. Crowninshield incredulously.

"It might. We have no way of knowing exactly what is raising the trouble."

"Do you mean to say that a storm that wasn't round here at all could——" burst out Jerry, then stopped embarrassed.

"Indeed it could," replied Bob, answering the unfinished question. "You see thunderstorms cause powerful electrical waves that affect apparatus miles and miles distant. Of course such waves vary in length but nevertheless they act on all aerials to a greater or less degree. Then, too, the atmospheric conditions are never quite identical, changing with the hour of the day, the season of the year, and local weather disturbances. Fortunately, since the air is positively electrified and the earth negatively, certain of these differences are remedied by the aerial that connects the two, the current discharges partially seeping off through the ground. Sometimes, however, in spite of every device used, such currents are strong enough to cause a roar in the receiver. In addition there is the interference from other radio stations which are busy transmitting messages, and although there are rules that aim to reduce this annoyance, it is, to a certain extent, always to be reckoned with."

"I should think somebody ought to invent something to prevent such troubles," declared Nancy.

"Why don't you, Sis?" asked Dick wickedly.

"But it is terrible to have the air so full of noise," continued the girl, as she made a little face at her brother. "I've always thought of the air as being still."

"It is still in a general sense," smiled Bob. "It is only when the amplifier of the wireless magnifies the sounds that we realize how many of them our ears fail to hear."

"It's a downright mercy they do!" exclaimed Jerry.

"You're right there, Jerry!" agreed Mr. Crowninshield.

"But how do messages come through such a chaos?" Dick inquired.

"Sometimes they don't," laughed Bob. "But nine cases out of ten they do because there are ways of combating static interference. You can, for instance, tune your apparatus to a higher or lower pitch and thereby escape from the zone where the noise is. That whine you hear is produced by my turning the tuning knob and increasing our range of meters. Already with the higher vibration you will notice the hubbub has lessened."

"Yes, things are ever so much clearer," agreed a chorus of voices.

"That is one way, then, out of the difficulty. There are, in addition, other mechanical means that can be resorted to when you learn more about handling the outfit. Suffice it to say that in a general way whatever tends toward inertia, or a lack of electrical activity, decreases static interference."

There was a pause in which above the crackling and the wailing of the instrument a faint sound became audible.

"Gee! Did you hear that?" cried Walter.

"Hush!"

"But I heard a voice quite distinctly."

"Keep still, can't you?" Dick remarked unceremoniously.

Then plainly into the room came the words:

"Station (WGI) Amrad Medford Hillside, Mass. 360 meters. Stand by for Boston Police reports."

"That is the police news," whispered Dick to Nancy. "Among other things it gives the automobiles that are lost, their numbers, and a description of each."

"Want to hear it?" asked Bob of his audience.

"Not unless they can tell us they have found Lola," responded Mr. Crowninshield promptly.

"Oh, no," his wife hastened to add, "let's not listen to a long string of crimes. Goodness knows there are enough of them to read in the papers."

She shook her head warningly at Bob and motioned toward her husband.

"I'd rather hear some music," put in Nancy. "Can't we?"

There was an ascending wail from the tuner.

"Ain't that a band?" cried Jerry excitedly.

"It's an orchestra!" Nancy ejaculated in the same breath.

"It's gone!"

"We'll get it again," was Bob's confident answer as he twirled the knobs of both tuner and detector.

"There it is!" burst out Jerry. "It's a brass band, as I live!"

"Where do you suppose it is?" speculated Mrs. Crowninshield.

"Pittsburgh or Chicago; or perhaps Newark."

"Not Chicago—out West! You're fooling," observed Jerry with scorn.

"Indeed I'm not. Wait and you'll hear in a few moments exactly who it was."

"I'll not believe it unless I do," the old man announced, with a zest that provoked a general laugh.

"What time is it? Can any one tell?" asked Bob.

"What difference does that make," Walter inquired.

"It will give us a cue as to who it is," was the explanation. "All these broadcasting stations have certain hours for their programs."

"I've seen those lists published in the papers, but I never took any stock in them," growled Jerry.

"You'll have to now, Jerry," said Nancy mischievously.

She saw him scratch his head.

"Well, I dunno," was his laconic reply. "The whole thing beats me. If that band was in Chicago——"

"Hush!"

The crash of instruments had come to an end and over the wire in accents unmistakably distinct came the words:

"Westinghouse Electric and Manufacturing Company KYW Chicago, Illinois. Stand by fifteen minutes for——" but the rest of the sentence was lost, for with a mighty slap of his knees Jerry roared:

"It was in Chicago—that band! Well, I'll be buttered!"

Overwhelmed the Cape Codder had risen to his feet.

"Chicago! Pittsburgh! Medford! My eye, but this will do me to talk about until the day of my death. It don't seem possible; I'm beat if it does."

Helplessly he dropped back into his chair again, silenced by very wonder.

In the meantime out of the wailing and whining and piping the sharp, clear-cut click of a telegraph instrument could be discerned.

"That's the Morse code," explained Bob. "Some commercial station is sending a message. It seems to be about a shipment of lumber and isn't particularly interesting."

"I suppose you can read it," said Dick enviously.

"Naturally. That is part of my job, you know."

"What is a commercial station?" inquired the still bewildered Jerry.

"A station that sends only messages for the general public. Probably this load of lumber started out of port without the captain of the ship having the least idea in the world where he was to market it. In the interval since it left, however, the company's shore agents have secured a customer for it, perhaps in New Bedford, Boston, Providence, or some other coast city and they are now notifying the ship where to deliver it. Such an arrangement is quite common nowadays. Were the captain obliged to hold his cargo in port until he had a purchaser, as was the usual rule in the past, he would be wasting much precious time. By this method he can set forth the moment the vessel is loaded and during his voyage let his managers search for buyers. In all probability by the time he nears New England harbors his wares will be sold and orders sent him where to deposit them."

"That's a neat little scheme!" observed Walter.

But poor Jerry was too much overcome by the marvels he had witnessed to comment on this added miracle. All he could do was to reiterate feebly: "It beats me—hanged if it don't!"

CHAPTER XVII

THE LAWS OF THE AIR

Morning found Mr. Crowninshield in no more tractable a mood. Even before Bob could reach his post at the wireless station and adjust his double head receiver to his ears his employer came briskly across the grass with his after-breakfast cigar between his lips.

"Well," began he, when he was within calling distance, "any news yet?"

"I'm afraid not yet, sir. It is still early."

The great man took out his watch.

"Isn't it almost time for O'Connel to signal?"

"It is nearing the time."

"I wonder if he will have any tidings for us?"

"I certainly hope so." The wish was uttered with deep sincerity. A speculation was forming in the young operator's mind as to how he was going to pacify the irascible gentleman before him should no tidings come.

"Since I'm here I believe I'll drop down and wait until you get into touch with the *Siren*."

"It is liable to be quite a little while. Sometimes there is delay."

"No matter. I've nothing especial to do to-day."

With sinking heart Bob turned away and began to fuss with his oil can and a bit of cotton waste.

"As you will, sir," was all he said.

"You think, don't you, that we will hear something definite this morning?"

"There is no telling."

"No, of course not. Nevertheless O'Connel can at least let us know whether Lola is worse or better."

"Yes, we ought to ascertain that."

"He wouldn't be such an idiot as to stand by and see the dog die, would he?"

"One never can predict just what another person will do. However, I feel sure you can trust O'Connel. I never knew him to bungle anything yet."

With that comfort Mr. Crowninshield was obliged to content himself.

Notwithstanding it, however, he began to pace nervously back and forth, and every time there was a sound in the room he would whisk about with the quick remark:

"Didn't you hear something?"

But although he fretted and fumed, strolled out the door and in again, no amount of impatience appeared to hurry matters.

Even Bob began to lose his poise and fear no message was coming when suddenly the well-known signal came and the familiar clockwork began to be clicked off.

"Is it he?" demanded Mr. Crowninshield in a tense whisper.

Bob nodded.

On clicked the code. Then suddenly it stopped and the man who was watching saw the operator raise the discs of rubber from his ears and shake himself free of his metal trappings.

"Well?" inquired Mr. Crowninshield in quick staccato.

"It was O'Connel. All he said was: *Wait developments.*"

"Not a word about Lola?"

"No, sir."

"Not a reference of any sort?"

"That was all."

"But that is no kind of a message," announced the exasperated owner of Surfside. "Why, it might mean almost anything."

"It sounds hopeful to me."

"I don't see any hope in it," was the despondent answer.

"At least it gives us to understand that something is brewing."

"But why couldn't he have told us more?"

"Perhaps he did not dare to. They may have begun to suspect he was sending private messages."

"Humph! I had not thought of that."

"Or possibly he may have been in a rush. He sent the letters at a tremendous pace—so fast that I had to race him. It seemed as if he was afraid he might not be able to get the message through."

"You didn't answer anything, I suppose."

"Only my signal to let him know I was listening."

"Then you think there is nothing more to be done at present but sit right here and see what happens?"

"I do not see how we can do anything else."

"It's frightfully annoying."

"Yes. Nevertheless it is our only course."

"You've no inkling whether the developments he mentioned are to be soon or not?"

"Not the ghost of an idea."

"Then there is nothing for it but to hold on right here a while longer, I'm afraid. And since we are all to be tied to the spot you may as well come up to the house later and give Dick his usual radio lesson."

"Very well, sir."

With a curt nod the financier went out the door and after

seeing that everything was right Bob locked up the building and followed him.

He found the little group assembled in the lee of the awnings waiting for him. Mr. Crowninshield was there, too, gnawing fiercely at a fresh cigar.

"I hear you have had a message, Bob," Mrs. Crowninshield said as he approached.

"Yes; a rather hopeful one, I think."

"I'm so excited! We all are. What do you suppose is in the wind?"

"I've no idea. Something good, I hope."

"Is that Morse code hard to learn?" inquired Nancy.

"The Morse Continental? That depends on what you consider hard," smiled Bob. "If your memory is good and you are quick at catching sounds it ought not to be very awful. Numberless persons do learn it."

"Of course sending messages after you have the code learned cannot be so bad, for you can take your own time," Dick put in. "It is receiving them that would fuss me."

"We'll fix you up with a buzzer and let you and Walter practice later if you want a try."

"Could you?" asked Dick eagerly.

"Sure! Moreover, there are phonograph records made on purpose to be used by beginners. Perhaps your father will get you some of those. It is a fine way to learn, training your ear to the sounds and giving you lots of practice."

"What a bully scheme!"

"It is a good proof of how one science can help another, isn't it?" observed Mrs. Crowninshield.

"I suppose transmitting is a great deal harder than receiving anyhow, isn't it?" pursued Dick.

"Well, of course there is more to it. In the rough it is merely the reverse of receiving; but in reality to project a message through the air requires a more elaborate outfit."

"But you said our wireless would send as well as receive."

"Oh, it will. It was made with both ends of the service in view. Your apparatus would first have to be adjusted and tuned until it was at the same frequency as the station with which you were talking. That you have to do anyhow, whether you are sending or receiving. And I told you, you remember, how to regulate that. Your antenna is connected through an adjustable induction coil, and moreover you have a small condenser which together with it forms a closed circuit. It is simple enough when you understand the principle to adjust the vibratory motion in the antenna by moving the connection. The frequency of the closed circuit can be adjusted, too. Tuning is nothing more than putting these two circuits into accord with the waves you receive. Your detector does a good part of the work for you, for it responds to every oscillation set up in the receiver. When, however, you are transmitting a message, you must take care to cut out your receiver by turning on the switch. Never forget that. You won't be likely to, either, when you are told why. You see it requires power to send out transmission waves and therefore to do it you have to employ a high-pressure current. Receiving, on the other hand, demands delicately adjusted instruments which are equipped to catch every faint, incoming wave. Should you let the strong charge of electricity used for transmission pass through your fragile receiving apparatus you would ruin it in no time."

"I can see that," replied Dick.

"Grasp that notion and you have one big principle of the difference between sending messages and receiving them," said Bob. "Skill in learning to take messages either in code or cipher comes with practice. The more you work at it the faster you can go. You have a keyboard all installed and the only thing standing between you and an expert operator is patience. Speed comes sooner than you think, too, if you practice persistently every day. As for the Morse code you press the key lever down quickly and instantly release it to make a dot. A dash is equal to three dots; the space between the parts of the same letters is equal to a dot; that between two letters to three dots; and between two words to five dots. You must train your ear until the span of these intervals becomes unmistakable. When you get some skill and are ready to try out what you can do, you will find that there are several ways of getting wider practice. There are, for example, local clubs that broadcast in code and send messages limited in speed to an amateur's capacity. Such centers are considerate enough to transmit at the rate of not more than five or ten words to the minute. It is persistence and a willingness to go slowly and carefully that win out in the end. A moderately delivered message that is without errors is worth a dozen fast, inaccurate ones; for when you blunder and have to go back and repeat, you not only waste your time and that of the man at the other end of the line but you annoy and usually confuse him. You will never gain anything if you are content with being a sloppy operator since above everything else radio messages must be correct. That is their chief value. Therefore, if after trying with all your might you find you cannot qualify as a topnotch, high-speed man be content to drop into the class below and be an accurate, slower operator. There are always certain things we do better than others. Speed may not be one of your gifts. That is no sign you have not other talents, however. Face the fact and go into the class where you belong. You won't get so nervous and fussed up, and by and by you may surprise yourself by finding that with time and experience the desired speed will come."

"I am not aiming to be a crackerjack like you," grinned Dick. "If I can take down and send any messages at all I shall feel pretty cocky."

"You think that now," returned Bob, ignoring the flattery contained in the observation. "But by and by you will find yourself discontented and as crazy to make time as you are in an automobile. There is a fascination about it."

"Doesn't the Morse Continental bother you a bit?" inquired Mr. Crowninshield.

"Not a particle. In fact, it has come to be almost as easy reading as straight English," answered Bob. "The thing that does fuss me sometimes though is to send and receive in cipher."

"Mercy! Do they do that too?" gasped Mrs. Crowninshield.

"Certainly. Often both in time of war and times of peace confidential messages which it is not desirable all the world should know have to be transmitted. Sometimes these are government communications; sometimes business or personal ones. At any rate, their senders wish them kept private and hence they are sent in cipher. Many of them are queer enough, too, when they come in."

"Can you understand them yourself?" asked Nancy.

"Certainly not. It is not intended that any one except the person for whom they are intended shall know what they mean."

"But I should think since they make no sense you would wonder whether you had them right," commented Dick.

"I do wonder sometimes," admitted Bob honestly. "When you get a sequence of queer words or combinations of letters you cannot help wondering. However, there is not much chance for a mistake, either in the transmission or in the delivery of such messages, for the operator is always obliged to send them slower than he does ordinary stuff, spacing the letters or groups of letters with unusual care. Furthermore, code words are always repeated once. This gives the man receiving them a chance to print the letters by hand rather than write them, a precaution that does much to prevent mistakes. The address and signature must also be very carefully transmitted. With such watchfulness at each end of the line it would be only a colossally stupid person who would blunder."

"But suppose the operator who is transmitting went faster than you could?" murmured Walter.

"He doesn't as a general rule. It isn't wireless ethics. And even should he be a more skillful radio man he knows he would gain nothing by hustling the chap at the other end for he would only lose time by having to go back and repeat."

"Is all the general transmission of messages given such care?" inquired Mr. Crowninshield.

"Of course cipher communications are fussier," Bob said. "Nevertheless the rules are pretty strict for all messages. And since accuracy is the keynote of radio and to get it your outfit must be in A1 condition, every care must be taken to have strong, clear, and effective sending and receiving power. That means you must constantly clean your apparatus and tighten it up; test out your detector by the buzzer intended for the purpose and make sure that it is in sensitive condition; and assure yourself that every part of your set is OK. Moreover, an operator who is on duty listening in is expected to wear the double head receiver all the time, so no sound, however faint, may get by him. He must also see that his detector is adjusted to its greatest degree of sensibility and his tuner to the proper wave length. If your station happens to be near another, or if you are one of a group of ships and other vessels near yours are sending, you must watch out and either weaken the coupling of your detector or open your switch and cut it out altogether when those around you are using powerful currents for transmission; else you will wreck this delicate part of your instrument."

"Gee, but there are things to remember!" ejaculated Dick.

"Not so many, really, if you use ordinary brains," Bob returned. "You just have to think, that is all. A few big principles hold throughout. The other *don'ts* are simply to make your own work and the other fellow's smoother; prevent mistakes; do away with as much interference as possible; and protect your outfit. For example, I found I could often lessen the interference by loosening the coupling of my receiving set after I had heard a call and reduce the sound to a point where it was just readable. You get your message all right but you do not get so much else with it. Then you can save wear and tear if you only run your generator while you are sending messages. That you cannot transmit at the hours reserved for naval radio stations to send out the time signals by which navigators set their chronometers, or when operators are broadcasting, goes without saying. Any dunce would know that."

"I had no idea there were hours for sending out the time," confessed Dick.

"Indeed there are. It is very important, too, that ships know the correct time to prevent disasters. There are shore stations whose sole duty it is to supply to ships the time and their location. Don't you recall my mentioning such coastal stations?"

"Oh, yes; I guess I do remember now," returned Dick, a trifle confused.

"What happens if you call a station and nobody answers?" interrogated Nancy. "I have been meaning to ask. Do you just keep on calling as you do at the telephone?"

"No, indeed," was the instant reply. "Should you do that you would cause no end of interference and make yourself a nuisance to everybody. The rule is that after you have called a station three times at two-minute intervals you must stop for a quarter of an hour before you call again. If you happened to be calling a fleet of ships it is desirable to alter your tune rather than keep repeating the summons in the same key. It saves time. Merchant ships and coast stations must, however, be called in the wave length definitely specified for their use."

"Shipboard stations seem to have more rules than the others," commented Dick.

"Not more rules but different ones," Bob said. "You see their nearness to other ships makes this imperative. Each ship has to take care not to knock out the apparatus of its neighbor by inconsiderate use of a high-power current; also it must not cause undue interference. In other words, a bevy of ships, like a group of persons, must be courteous to one another. If a ship within a ten-mile radius of another is receiving signals that are so faint that they are difficult to distinguish, a neighboring vessel should not complicate matters by trying to transmit a message until the other ship has received what was coming in. This rule makes for ordinary politeness, that is all."

"Couldn't the ship waiting to talk send a message in a different wave length?" inquired Dick.

"Oh, yes; that would be quite possible, if the tune varied enough to make it perfectly distinct."

"But what about high-power stations?" demanded Walter. "They handle important stuff and of course cannot keep stopping for other people to talk. Don't their powerful currents damage the receiving sets in stations near them? I should think they might even injure their own."

"High-power, or long-distance stations have still another problem to meet and they meet it in a different way," responded Bob. "In order that the currents they are obliged to use shall not destroy detectors and other delicate receiving apparatus they carry on what are known as duplex operations. That is, the receiving station is constructed at some distance from the sending station—often several miles away—and the two parts of the service are performed independently by different antennæ. In this way sending and receiving can be carried on at the same time in slightly varying wave lengths."

"But how can they talk and act as one station if they are so far apart?" questioned His Highness much puzzled.

"It is not as impossible as it seems. The operator at the sending station has a small sending key connected by electricity with a relay at the receiving station. By means of a lever and certain complex paraphernalia this key can be used as the sending key for the main apparatus. Thus the station operated by distant control carries on a duplex system of transmission so that both sending and receiving stations are kept in touch with one another."

"That is clever!" interrupted Mr. Crowninshield.

"A high-power station has to be ingeniously equipped," responded Bob, "for it does a great deal of business, rapid business and business that is important. In some stations so fast do the messages come in and so long are they that an automatic tape not unlike that seen at the stock exchange is used to make perforated records of the dots and dashes. Later this punctured slip can be run through a Morse writer and the message taken down at leisure by the operator. Or sometimes photographic or phonographic records are resorted to and these like the others can be reproduced at a slower rate of speed and interpreted by the operator."

"I should like that and then I wouldn't have to hurry," murmured Nancy.

"It must be jolly to be an operator in a long-distance station," mused Dick, "where real things are going on."

"Perhaps it is," was Bob's nonchalant answer. "I fancy, though, that very vital government messages go in cipher. Uncle Sam isn't risking having his secrets published far and wide over the face of the whole earth. Although for that matter all radio messages are secret."

"But how can they be if any and everybody can listen in?"

"Well, on a high-power wave length probably ordinary persons would not be able to listen in. Their apparatus would not be equipped for it. Should a station be able to, however, during critical periods, such as times of war, the government takes no chances and orders all but certain specified stations dismantled. That puts an end to intruders unless a spy has a hidden wireless somewhere; and if he has he takes an almighty risk with his neck, that is all I can say," concluded Bob with a grin.

"But operators have tongues and can talk," Mrs. Crowninshield suggested. "Don't they sometimes?"

"Usually they do not know what the message passing through their hands means," Bob answered. "But even should they contrive to study it out they would not dare repeat it because of the penalty entailed."

"Penalty?"

The young operator nodded.

"You would not have to concern yourself much about blabbers if you heard what happens to them," piped Walter, who suddenly found himself on ground which previous instruction had rendered familiar. "It's off with their heads!"

"Not really!" gasped the horrified Nancy.

"Oh, he does not mean literally," the elder brother explained. "But it is away with their license which is almost as disastrous a fate to a man who has planned to make his living by wireless. Nor is the loss of the license all that happens. In addition one is liable to a two-hundred-and-fifty-dollar fine or three years' imprisonment."

"Jove! They do come down on you!" Dick averred.

"Ra-*ther*! You know, of course, that if you violate any clause of your radio agreement you may be fined one hundred dollars; and should an operator fake a distress call the fine is twenty-five hundred dollars, or five years in prison and perhaps both. Even the smallest fine one can get off with for such an offense is two years behind the bars. It makes you think twice before playing that little joke. The government is wise, too, to spread it on thick, for to fake an S O S which is given the right of way over every other signal would be a contemptible trick. Mild punishments like fines and imprisonments would be too good for the wretch who would so deliberately mislead people. Moreover a few such offenses would cause the importance of the call to be discredited so that in time nobody would be in a rush to pay attention to it."

"I didn't realize an S O S so invariably had the right of way," meditated Dick. "Of course I knew it was the distress signal at sea."

"S O S in the International Morse Code is the universal distress call adopted by the common consent of our civilized nations at the wireless convention held at Berlin in 1906. Every radio station ashore or afloat is obliged to give it first place and do everything possible to further its demands. When a distress call is heard all ships and stations everywhere that hear it are in honor bound to stop whatever they may be doing and listen; nor must they try to talk with the ship herself unless she asks them to. Instead, after she has sent out her call for attention, which is equivalent to our *Hello* of the telephone, she gives her name; the name of the station or ship she wishes to talk with; states what the matter is; and defines as nearly as she is able her position. This done she sends out a general call and if the station or ship she has asked aid from has not caught the signal and fails to answer her, any operator within hearing may do so. The instant he begins to talk with her, however, all the others listening in must remain silent. At last, when the message is delivered or the necessary conversation at an end, then the ship's radio man sends out a broadcast to let everybody know that he has finished so that all stations may resume their regular routine."

"Some system!" breathed Dick.

"I guess you would think there was some system if you were to see a book of radio rules," returned Bob. "I'll show you mine some day. All the various shore stations have their many regulations, as I have told you before; shipboard stations have theirs; and even the amateurs are protected so that every class may get fair play and not bother his neighbor. Wireless stations, you see, are not mere toys. They have work to do and must be able to do it unhampered."

"I'd like a glimpse of that manual," suggested Dick.

"I'll bring it round to-morrow," Bob answered, glancing at his watch and rising.

The others rose too.

"I suppose it would be no use to listen in for O'Connel again," remarked Mr. Crowninshield.

"I will if you like," Bob responded. "I doubt, though, if it would do any good."

"No, I guess it wouldn't. We shall just have to wait," sighed the man.

CHAPTER XVIII

THE NET TIGHTENS

When on the morrow no call of any kind came from O'Connel Mr. Crowninshield was, as his son expressed it, "fit to be tied."

"I can't see why we do not hear something to-day," fumed he. "He can't expect us to *wait developments* forever. Are you sure you did not miss the signal, Bob."

"I don't see how I could have missed it," replied the operator patiently.

"But he always does call, doesn't he?"

"He has for the last few days."

"Then why not to-day?"

"I cannot imagine. Perhaps he couldn't."

"You don't suppose anything has happened to Lola, do you?"

"Who can tell?"

"You are right; it was a foolish question," admitted the financier, accepting the rebuke gracefully. "Still, I cannot help being anxious and wondering."

"Of course not."

"If only that miserable inspector would turn up and you could get your license! It is absurd that you cannot send a message, a man of your experience!"

"I am as sorry about the delay as you are," Bob answered.

"Perhaps I am more so. Nevertheless I am not going to break the rules. Besides, were we to call O'Connel, it might arouse suspicion and get him into trouble. It is far better to leave the calling to him."

"But he hasn't called."

"Then there is some good reason, I'll be bound. He knows what he is about when he says to await developments."

"Maybe he does," sighed the elder man. "However, I am not much used to waiting. When I want a thing done, I want it done."

Bob smiled at the characteristic remark.

"You cannot whisk everything off like that," observed he. "Sometimes it is necessary——"

"To wait? Yes, I suppose so," put in Mr. Crowninshield. "Well, I will hold my horses for one more day. But I warn you to-morrow I shall do something. I can't be hanging around like this—not knowing anything or hearing anything."

"It is hard," Bob returned sympathetically.

"It is hard for one born in New York and accustomed to seeing things hum," asserted the owner of Surfside with a wry smile. "Well, we must try to forget it, that's all. Come, get your books and let us go on with our radio lesson from the point where we left it yesterday. The rest of them are waiting and there seems to be nothing better that we can do."

Fortunately Bob was not sensitive enough to be hurt by the thrust.

"I'll be right along," agreed he, "as soon as I have locked up here."

On reaching the veranda he found his class assembled and the first comment to reach his ears was:

"No news from O'Connel, eh?"

"No, Dick."

"What in thunder do you suppose has become of him?"

Bob put his finger to his lips and taking the hint the boy abandoned the subject, inquiring instead:

"Isn't it a bore to have to listen in at just such a time every day whether it is convenient or not—I mean when you are in charge of a station."

"Sometimes it is," Bob responded. "Still, it is your job and you expect to put it first and fit your own affairs in around it. Besides, you get used to the regularity of the hours and soon do not notice the monotony of the rules. You can readily understand why, at all official radio stations, somebody must always be on the watch for S O S calls. On shipboard there are three classes of wireless stations: those having continual service with an operator who always has his ear to the receiver while the ship is in motion; those where the office is open only at stated hours and an operator listening merely for a limited time; and those whose operators have no fixed time beyond listening in the first ten minutes of each hour."

"The ship decides which kind of station it will have, I suppose," Nancy remarked.

"Indeed it doesn't," Bob contradicted, with a shake of his head. "The government saves the vessel that trouble. It defines exactly the sort of station when it issues the license. Uncle Sam also bestows on each of these stations a name or combination of letters by which it shall be known and under which it is officially listed. Each country has a prescribed number of such letters allotted for its use at the International Convention at Berne, and our nation is authorized to use groups beginning with N and W; also triple groups of KIA to KZZ. You will find all these call letters in a book that contains the wireless telegraph stations of the world, a volume issued by the international publication office at Berne."

"Can any one get one?" inquired Walter.

"Certainly, if he has the price," smiled the older brother. "I guess you do not need one, though. A local call book would answer most purposes. It would hardly be necessary for you to call any foreign offices, and I even doubt if you would need to summon Sayville, Tuckerton, New Brunswick, Marion, or Annapolis."

"Those are our trans-Atlantic stations, aren't they?" asked Dick.

"Some of them," Bob said. "We have others, though, that can talk with Europe. There is one at San Diego; Pearl Harbor in Hawaii; and Cavite in the Philippines. There are also Marconi stations at Kahuka and Bolinas. In addition to these, the government has a number of high-power stations scattered throughout the country. Arlington, Virginia——"

"Sends out the time," put in Walter with disconcerting promptness.

"It sure does, sonny."

"How many foreign countries can talk with us?" inquired Nancy.

"A short time ago there were eight that could talk direct. One is at Funabashi, Japan; one at Carnarvon, Wales; two in France, one at Nantes and one at Lyons; Rome, Italy, has one; Germany has one at Nauen and one at Eilvese, Hanover; and Norway has one at Stavanger. Then in Canada there are two transatlantic stations."

"Glace Bay!" piped the incorrigible Walter.

Bob patted his head with a mock fatherly gesture.

"Very good, son," said he, at which everybody laughed.

"These stations," he went on, "are all equipped with very high power, varying in wave length anywhere from 17,600 to 6,000 meters. Most of our stations are pretty powerful, anyway. Pearl Harbor, for instance, has a 13,000 wave length; Cavite 12,000; Sayville, 11,600; Tuckerton, owned by a French company, about 8,700; New Brunswick, New Jersey, 13,600; Marion, Massachusetts, 14,400; and Annapolis, 17,600. Only a few foreign stations can match these in range. Carnarvon has two wave lengths: 14,000 and 11,500; Lyons, 15,500; Nantes, 10,000; Rome, 11,500; Nauen, 12,550; Eilvese (Hanover), 15,000 and 9,600; and Stavanger, Norway, 9,600. There are many, however, that vary from 7,000 to 4,000 and can transmit messages by relaying them."

"I wish my set could send farther," Dick murmured regretfully.

"It sends as far as the law allows. We must therefore abide by Uncle Sam's judgment and be content. The scale is very carefully planned and the classifications made most intelligently, I think. Amateurs are limited to about a 200-meter wave length; low-power stations come next and are grouped under 1,600 meters. Of these the 750 wave is reserved for government stations such as radio compass stations, etc.; 600 meters is the commercial tune for large merchant ships; 476 that of submarines, aircraft, and small war vessels; and 300 meters is the commercial tune for small vessels. After that we pass into the higher group, all of which come under the head of medium-power stations. These range from 4,000 to 1,800 meters and first on the list are the government ships which have continuous waves and a length of from 3,000 to 4,000 meters. Following them come the experimental and miscellaneous stations with a 3,000 to 2,000-meter range; and after them the 1,800-meter class which is the commercial tune for continuous waves."

"And the high-power stations are the last, I suppose," put in Dick.

"Yes, those designed for trans-oceanic service. These range from 20,000 to 6,000 meters. The distinctions are, you see, quite positively made and everybody must keep within his assigned pigeon-hole."

"I reckon I'll keep in mine," announced Dick.

"I should advise it if you want smooth sailing," retorted Bob. "You will hardly——" but the sentence was never finished for a maid approached Mr. Crowninshield at the moment and whispered:

"The telephone, sir; New York is speaking."

"New York, Dad!" exclaimed Dick excitedly. "It may be Lyman or Dacie."

"More likely it is the office," replied his mother.

"Some business matter, I fancy," said Mr. Crowninshield as he rose. "I'm sorry to interrupt the lesson."

"I was just about through, sir."

"I'll be back in a moment probably."

"Poor father always has telephone calls," lamented Nancy sympathetically. "If he ever starts out to play golf somebody is sure to want him. Sometimes I wish that New York office was in the bottom of the sea."

"I guess you'd have precious little bread and butter if it was," announced Dick with brotherly sarcasm.

"Certainly you wouldn't be able to provide me with any," Nancy flashed back with a teasing laugh.

"Children!" interposed Mrs. Crowninshield.

"Here's Dad! Well, Pater, what was it?" asked Dick. Then on observing his father was unwontedly excited he repeated, "What's up, Dad?"

"It was Lyman," Mr. Crowninshield answered. "The New York police have run down two men and Mr. Lyman wants

Bob to come over and see if he can identify either of them as the one who kidnapped Lola."

"You could identify him, couldn't you, Bob?" Walter put in.

"Of course I could. Didn't the chap come into the station to get water for his machine?" was the instant reply. "I talked with him quite a bit while he was fixing up his engine. He seemed in a powerful rush to be off and wasn't overgracious."

"But could Bob leave now, Archibald?" questioned his wife. "Isn't there the possibility of news from Mr. O'Connel?"

"Jove! I had forgotten that."

"Maybe O'Connel won't call; he didn't to-day, you know," Nancy said.

"It seems to me Bob ought to go and land those chaps if there is a chance of doing it," Dick declared. "He would not need to be gone more than one night, would he?"

"No. Nevertheless, he would miss the morning wireless," returned Mr. Crowninshield. "Should there be important news we should not get it."

"It is a pity you boys can't take a message," Nancy remarked, turning toward her brother and Walter. "If you only had your Morse code learned you might be quite some good to us now."

"I wish I had whooped up on it faster," bewailed Dick, with engaging candor. "I'm an awful rotter—plain lazy, I guess."

"Well, I don't know but we'd better let Bob go, all things considered," observed Mr. Crowninshield, who had been quietly thinking the matter over.

"I say Bob goes, too," reiterated Dick. "It is worth something to put such fellows as those dog thieves behind the bars."

"You can connect with the Fall River boat or one passing through the Canal and be in New York in the morning, Bob," the elder man asserted. "Lyman will meet you, hustle things along, and send you home on the noon train. With Dick's racing car to pick you up somewhere along the line there is no reason why we should not have you back here before another morning. You've no time to spare, though, for lingering and discussing wireless and its wonders. Trot along and pack up your duds and get some luncheon. I'll call up Wheeler and have him ready to carry you to the train. Do not bother your head about connections; I will look up everything and tell you exactly what to do."

In a flurry of anticipation off hastened Bob.

"Gee! Isn't it the limit that we haven't brains enough to get O'Connel?" murmured Dick to Walter in a disgusted whisper. "I ought to have duffed in harder on the blamed code. But I thought there was no hurry. We seemed to have all summer to learn it."

"Maybe he won't call," His Highness suggested hopefully.

"I hope to blazes he doesn't," was the retort. "I'd feel cheap as dirt to have that ticker go clicking out a message and I not be able to get a word of it."

CHAPTER XIX

WALTER STEPS INTO THE BREACH

With Bob gone and radio lessons suspended the following morning seemed to both Dick and Walter an unwontedly quiet one. Moreover with a scorching sun high in the heaven, no breeze, and a dead low tide most of the activities to which the boys might have resorted were out of the question.

"Think of the sailing breeze we've seen blowing lots of mornings when we couldn't go out," grumbled Dick. "Isn't it infernal luck?"

"Why don't you take your car and go for a spin," Nancy suggested.

"Wheeler has it, silly. He's meeting Bob."

"I couldn't go motoring anyway," put in Walter. "I've got the dogs to chase round."

"You're not going out with them now," objected Dick.

"Not quite yet. I had them out before breakfast."

"What do you say we go over and fool round with the radio a while?" Dick yawned. "We've nothing better to do."

"All right. We can at least listen in for a spell. We've got that far."

"You boys better not go getting that wireless all out of order while Bob is away," cautioned Nancy. "He'd be ripping mad to get home and find it out of commission. Father wouldn't like it, either."

"Oh, we're not going to hurt the precious radio," sniffed Dick. "Don't you think we know anything?"

"Not much," fluted Nancy as she flounced away.

"At least she does not flatter us," grinned His Highness, quite unruffled by the girl's frankness.

"Oh, sisters never think a fellow knows anything, especially when they're older," Dick grumbled, as he unlocked the door of the low building and met the blast of close, stifling air that came out. "Scott! The place is like an oven, isn't it? Open a window, can't you?" he continued.

"Sure! There is some heat, I'll say. Just as well we dropped round if only to air the place out," Walter replied.

Together they switched on the current, regulated amplifier, detector, and tuner, and each with a head receiver tight to his ears sat down.

"Whee, but it is thick, to-day!" shouted Dick. "Run the tune up, kid, and see if we get anything."

"It is always bad on a day like this," called Walter. "Besides, everybody seems to be butting in in the morning. Infernal, isn't it?"

"Let her go up to O'Connel's pitch. It can't do any harm."

"It isn't time for him to call, is it?"

"Pretty near."

"But what good would it do even if we did get his signal?"

"We should at least know he had something to say to us."

"I should consider that a negative satisfaction," Walter replied. "It would just be an aggravation. However, here she goes! As you say, it can harm nobody to get the right meter."

CLEARLY AND EVENLY THE MESSAGE TICKED ITSELF OFF.
THEN THERE WAS SILENCE.

"There's that old commercial station up the Cape," announced Dick, presently. "That fellow is always on the job at this hour."

"Probably he has to be, poor soul," Walter returned. "We'll get rid of him in a minute. *What was that?*"

"It is some one on our line. That's the *Siren's* call. It's O'Connel! Jove! What are you doing, man? What are you going to do?" asked Dick excitedly as he saw Walter's hand go out.

"Paper! Pencil! Hurry, can't you?" gasped Walter.

"Do you mean——"

"Let's both take it down in dots and dashes. Between us we may be able to make some sense out of it afterward. Quick!"

Clearly and evenly the message ticked itself off. Then there was silence.

"Get any of it?" Walter demanded, breathlessly tossing the receiver aside and shutting off the current.

"About two words. He went so fast——Did you get anything?"

"Oh, I've got something; but whether it will make any sense remains to be seen," said His Highness eagerly. "Where is the key! Toss it over."

"Here we go. Dot, dash,——"

"That's the letter A, you squarehead! I know what that first part is; it is always the same and we needn't fuss to translate it. *Aboard yacht Siren.* I don't care, either, where she is. What we want to get at is what she wants to say."

"But how can we tell where all that stuff leaves off?"

"I mean to tell," declared Walter with determination.

"But there is punctuation and other rubbish mixed in with the letters."

"No matter. Have a little patience, man!"

Nevertheless, in spite of all the patience and perseverance the boys could muster, the magic message remained an enigma and at the end of an hour both were obliged to admit themselves beaten.

"It is worse than getting no message at all," lamented Walter.

"It certainly does not do us much good," assented Dick.

"Do you suppose your father knows anything about the Morse code?"

"Dad? Good heavens, no! Still we might take the thing up to the house and show it to him."

"I don't imagine it is right, do you?" speculated Walter. "No doubt we missed some of it or made mistakes. Still, what we contrived to write agrees fairly well, so some of it must be correct. Let's take it to your father. What do you say?"

"I feel like such a boob not to be able to make it out," Dick answered with evident reluctance at confessing himself floored.

"But we'll have to tell him O'Connel called. We've got to do that anyhow; so he may as well know the rest of it," Walter persisted.

"All right. We'll hunt him up. I warn you, though, that he will josh us most unmercifully. He'll pitch into me, too, and ask me why I haven't learned my Morse International before this. See if he doesn't."

"It is one thing to learn the code out of a book and quite another to be smart enough to read it or take it down," Walter maintained stoutly. "Nobody ought to expect you to be able to get a message the way Bob does. Why, he has been at the job years!"

"I know he has," Dick responded, slightly comforted. "Still, Dad will rag me, just the same. See if he doesn't!"

Locking the door and pausing to gain courage they set out over the lawn. Then suddenly, midway across the grass, His Highness came to a stop.

"Mr. Burns!" he cried, wheeling round. "Why didn't I think of him before?"

"What on earth are you talking about?" asked Dick, astounded by his companion's strange conduct.

"Mr. Burns!" repeated Walter. "Come along. Can't one of the chauffeurs take us down there?"

"For mercy's sake who is Mr. Burns, and why do you want to go and see him hot off the bat?"

"Mr. Burns, the telegraph operator," Walter contrived to stammer. "He must know Morse International. He has to know both the Morse American which telegraph operators use on land, and the other code, I'm pretty sure."

"But maybe what we've got down doesn't make sense," objected Dick. "You've a husky nerve to go toting that scrawl of ours to a professional."

"I don't care," grinned Walter. "I'm not afraid of Mr. Burns. He's driven me out of the station too many times when I was a kid. I will own, however, that I have more respect for him since I've learned what it means to run a telegraph."

"He may drive you out of the station this time," Dick ventured with a grimace.

"I'll bet he won't," was the sanguine response. "We've made it up since then. I've even helped old Burnsie shovel his snow now and then. He'll do a good turn for me, I'll bet."

"Come on then, if you are so sure of it," Dick answered, striding toward the garage.

"You're sure your father won't mind our taking the car?"

"He doesn't want it this morning. He is going to hang round and see if Bob calls him from New York. Besides, he said it was too hot to motor. Will Burns be at the station now?"

"He will if a train is due," announced Walter. "If the office is locked we can chase him to his house."

"All right! This is your party, remember," Dick said a trifle wickedly. It was evident he had no faith in the expedition. Notwithstanding his skepticisms, however, he ordered out the car and he and Walter sped away on their errand.

"It is time for a train," announced Walter in an undertone, as they neared the station. "See, there are people waiting. It is the noon train from Boston."

"Burns will be too busy then to bother his head over fake messages, I guess," sniffed Dick.

"Maybe not. At least we can try him," was His Highness's optimistic assertion. "Hi, Mr. Burns!" The lad was out of the car and hastening along in the wake of a much sunburned station agent in blue denim overalls.

"Wal, if it ain't Walter King! What you after, young one? I hear you've become the proprietor of Surfside—bought out the whole darn place for yourself."

"I did buy it but I'm going to sell it again. It's too small. I can't get room enough to stretch up there," came impishly from the lad on the platform.

"Show! You don't say!" drawled Mr. Burns with obvious relish of the joke. "Well, it ain't wise to be cramped. Maybe you wouldn't get your growth if you were."

He cast a glance toward the short, thick-set figure behind him.

"I say, Mr. Burns," burst out Walter, "are you terribly busy? I've got something I want to show you."

"What is it?" demanded the man, halting and holding suspended in his hand a cerulean blue egg case.

"I don't know what it is—that's just the trouble," answered Walter mysteriously.

"What you up to anyhow?" demanded Mr. Burns suspiciously.

Walter thrust forth the sheet of paper he had drawn from his pocket.

In his rough, grimy hand the telegraph operator took it.

"Where did you get this?" demanded he, glancing sharply over the top of his spectacles.

"Why, we have a wireless up at Surfside and this thing—or something like it that we didn't know enough to write down, came this morning."

"But I heard your brother Bob was up there."

"He had to go to New York yesterday."

"And left you to tend the tape, did he?" grinned the old man.

"Not much. He knows I'd be a duffer at the job," affirmed Walter.

"Mebbe you ain't as much of a duffer as you think. You managed to get this down on paper."

"We managed to together—Dick and I," explained Walter. "I don't suppose, though, we got it anywhere near straight. Does it make any sense at all?"

"Sure it makes sense!" announced Mr. Burns with a vim that quite took Walter's breath away. "There's queer spots in it here and there—a few letters that ain't needed, perhaps. Still, you can omit 'em since they serve no particular purpose."

"But what is the message? What does it say?" clamored Walter all impatience.

"Well, it ain't so thrillin' you need to go into a thousand pieces over it," commented the Cape Codder dryly. "Some friend of Mr. Crowninshield's 'pears to be comin' down here on the afternoon train bringin' with him his wife—either his wife or daughter."

"What!" Walter ejaculated weakly.

"That's what he says," continued Mr. Burns, calmly rereading the document he held. "Evidently some relation—or at least a person who feels he has the right to boss, for he says he wants to be met at the train."

"Did I get the name?"

"Yes, that's here. I may's well read you the whole thing with the exception of the extra touches you've added."

"I wish to goodness you would."

"'Tain't nothin' interestin', as I said before," insisted Mr. Burns, readjusting his spectacles. "'*Coming on afternoon train and bringing Lola. Meet me, O'Con——*' Where in thunder you goin'?" The operator gazed in amazement as a pair of chubby legs vanished up the platform.

"That's all right, Mr. Burns! I don't want the paper back. You can keep it to remember me by. Thanks!" Then to Dick he shouted as he sprang into the car:

"We're off for home fast as we can make it, old man! Such news! Your father will be crazy! Whee! Hurrah!"

"If it is all the same to you," observed Dick with scorching sarcasm, "it would be pleasant to know the import of the message I took down."

"*You* took down—well I like that! *You* took down! Why, man, you could not even read it yourself! It is the message *I* took down, my son."

"*We* took down," corrected Dick.

They both laughed.

"O'Connel's coming this afternoon! What do you say to that?"

"Great Scott! But what——"

"He's bringing his wife or daughter," continued Walter with a wicked twinkle in his eye.

"What?" exclaimed his bewildered listener.

"Oh, this is rich! Rich!" continued His Highness with a paroxysm of laughter. "Wait until we tell your father! My soul and body! I'm sick laughing!"

"You might tell me the joke."

"I can't—I can't!" roared the boy. "It is too good!"

"And—and what about Lola?" stammered Dick.

"Why, you see Burns thought—my, but it's rich! Ha, ha! Burns understood that—oh, it's a scream!" and with that Dick was forced to be content.

CHAPTER XX

THE RETURN OF THE WANDERERS

When Walter and Dick returned to Surfside with their tidings, Mr. Crowninshield's satisfaction and delight could hardly be expressed. How he laughed at Burns's interpretation of O'Connel's message! And how Dick laughed when at last the joke was imparted to him!

"Well, you two boys have been almighty clever between you," commented the elder man. "I would not have credited either of you with so many brains. To think of your getting that radio call! It is marvelous. And then to take it to Burns! That was a master stroke. The idea would never have entered my head. But what puzzles me is the message itself. Do you suppose O'Connel has kidnapped Lola; or how has he got possession of her? And how has he contrived to escape from the yacht without being held up? I don't understand it at all. It isn't likely Daly has let him walk off unmolested with the dog. The thing is more than I can fathom."

"Perhaps Mr. Daly has relented and is sending Lola back," suggested Walter.

"Not on your life, youngster! You don't know Daly," was the instant reply. "He would never admit himself beaten and give up that pup. Moreover the affair has cost him too much money, risk and trouble for him to abandon his scheme. If he wanted Lola bad enough to hire somebody to steal her he still wants her, mark my word! No, there is something behind all this that we haven't reached. O'Connel has made off with the dog somehow. Just how I am at a loss to tell. We shall have to wait until he himself comes and enlightens us."

"Anything heard from Bob?" questioned Walter.

"Yes, I've had a wire. They've got the men they were after all right and he will be back to-night."

"What did he say about it?" asked Dick eagerly.

"Nothing. You cannot tell an entire story in a telegram, you know. But he has accomplished what he went for. I fancy he always does," added the master of the estate with a smile.

"Generally, sir," nodded Walter proudly.

Mr. Crowninshield took a turn or two across the room.

"I mean to keep Bob with us this winter if I can prevail upon him to stay," remarked the financier presently. "He is too able a chap to lose sight of. I can find a big paying berth for him in New York and if he will take it, your mother won't have to worry any further about money affairs. And if you, sonny, make good and do as well as your brother"—he patted Walter's shoulder, "I'll do the same for you some day. You have done well this summer. Finish up your school work and then we'll see."

"You are very kind, Mr. Crowninshield," the boy stammered.

"Not a bit. We all ought to give the chap who is willing to climb a hand up the ladder. What are we in the world for?"

"I know my mother will be———"

"There, there!" interrupted the great man. "Your mother has two fine sons that she may well be proud of. She has had a little hard sledding to get them on their feet, that's all. Now it is their turn to lift the burden and repay her. I am simply going to see that they get the chance to do it. The rest I feel certain I can leave to them."

"We do want to help mother," Walter replied with sincerity.

"I know you do; both of you have proved it this summer. From now on I intend your mother shall have no anxiety about her finances. We'll put her where she will be perfectly independent of those uncles of yours, and of summer boarders as well."

The lip of His Highness trembled and he could not speak.

"Some day I expect Dick and Nancy will be looking out for their mother and me just this way," continued Mr. Crowninshield half humorously. "There will be Lola to support, too."

Dick burst into a peal of laughter.

"You will have to cut out indulging in so many detectives if I'm to pay the bills, Dad," answered he.

"Oh, you must not deprive me of my little luxuries," returned his father. "One must have some amusement, remember."

"I'm afraid you will have to choose a cheaper one then."

"I'll think it over. If, however, I discover you cannot maintain me and my trifling pleasures I may abandon you and turn to Walter to support me in my old age."

Lighting a cigar he strolled away.

The boys ambled toward the boathouse. There was still three hours before the Boston train, bringing O'Connel, would arrive. In the meantime they indulged in a swim; took the dogs for a run; had luncheon; paddled round the bay in Dick's canoe; and did everything they could think of to hurry the moments along.

And when the car bearing Mr. Crowninshield and O'Connel did actually roll into the drive what a state of excitement they were in!

Yes, there was Lola—there was no contesting that! She was a weak, wretched little dog but it was she.

"However did you manage it, Mr. O'Connel?" cried Mrs. Crowninshield who had come racing down the steps and gathered her favorite into her arms.

Breathlessly the group clustered about the wee puppy.

"Well, the first thing I did was to convince myself the dog aboard the yacht was really the one we were after. One day when the party went ashore I hunted up the supposed Trixie and called her by her real name. You should have seen her prick up her ears, poor little mite! I had her licking my hand inside a minute. From that instant I began to scheme. I found I couldn't send you many radio calls because they watched me too closely. I think the mate suspected something—just what, I could not make out, for I don't think he was in the secret of the dog's capture. Anyway, I decided to steer clear of the wireless and trust to luck. At last my chance came. Some equipment was needed and it was decided I was to be put ashore and get it. By this time Lola, who for the last few days had refused to eat, had begun to show decidedly alarming symptoms. I diagnosed the case as plain homesickness and privately resolved to get her off the yacht if it was a possible thing; but Mr. Daly thought she had distemper or something and was mightily cut up. He didn't want the animal to die on his hands after all he had gone through to get her. Altogether he began to be pretty uneasy and you may be sure I did my part to make him so. Every chance I got I would remark how sick his dog seemed. Of course I wasn't supposed to know it wasn't one he had had for years. I kept harping on the puppy's health until I had him fussed to death. At last he said: 'I don't know but what you are right about Trixie, O'Connel. If they are going to put you ashore at Boston to buy supplies, why wouldn't it be a good plan for you to take the dog to the animal hospital there? You could leave her and later we could go back and get her.

She does seem ailing, and I haven't the ghost of an idea what to do with a sick dog. Besides, she is a nuisance on the yacht if she must be catered to all the time.' Well, as you can imagine, I jumped at the chance although I took every pains not to let him suspect I did. I told him that of course if he wanted me to take the dog I should be glad to do it. I liked animals and also I wished to accommodate him. There was no denying, however, that to carry Lola with me would delay me in town. Still, if he desired it I would do my best to see that she was taken *where she would get well.*"

The big fellow paused and laughed heartily.

"I've kept that promise, too," grinned he. "I have sent a note back to the *Siren* recalling the phrase to Mr. Daly, and telling him that having decided Lola would recover more completely if placed under the protection of her rightful owners I was taking her back there."

"I'd like to see his face when he gets that letter!" said Mr. Crowninshield, rubbing his hands.

"So should I," roared O'Connel, his broad shoulders shaking.

"But won't he——" Mrs. Crowninshield looked anxious.

"Won't he what, my dear?" inquired her husband.

"Aren't you afraid he will be angry and——" she held the wee dog closer in her arms.

"He will be angry all right," agreed O'Connel. "But you need have no fears that he will do anything more, ma'am. He is on too dangerous ground. In the first place he cannot accuse me of appropriating his dog for I can answer him that it was stolen in the first place. And he cannot say I deserted his ship for all is fair in love and war, you know. No, Daly is a good sport and he will instantly understand that he has been beaten. We have been one too many for him, that is all. Moreover, he won't be feeling any too comfortable for he is still uncertain as to what Mr. Crowninshield may be planning to do with him. Oh, Daly won't stir up trouble. You can trust him for that. On the contrary he probably will clear out of reach of any possible storm. It is his only course and he will be canny enough to take it."

"But you are not going to let him go scott free, are you Dad?" demanded Dick.

"Oh, I don't know. What's the use of fighting a skunk like that? We have our dog back and Daly must acknowledge that he has been beaten. That is about all I want. He won't try anything more for I have a whiplash over him as he is well aware. Any time I can prosecute him for receiving stolen goods and being an accomplice in a robbery. With the evidence I have such a case would go overwhelmingly against him should it reach the courts. He is not for bringing that issue to a head, you may rest assured of that."

"But you do mean to jail the men who actually took Lola, Father," put in Nancy. "If you do that, won't the whole affair have to be aired and Mr. Daly dragged into the trial?"

Her father did not answer immediately and before he had framed his reply wheels were heard and Wheeler, driving Dick's racing car, drew up at the steps.

"It's Bob, as I live!" shouted Walter. "Hello, Bobbie! Hello, old chap!"

"Welcome home, Bob!" called Mr. Crowninshield going forward to meet the lad.

"We have a surprise for you, Bob!" called Nancy. "Guess who's here?"

"I can't," smiled the wireless man coming up to the piazza and shaking hands all round. Then his eye lighted on O'Connel.

"My word! How did you get here, old top? Fired from your job?"

For answer Mrs. Crowninshield held up Lola.

"The pup herself! Well, well! What's been happening in my absence, anyhow?"

"I don't wonder you want to know," cried Nancy above the general clamor.

"Hush! Do stop everybody. You are making a far worse noise than ever came through that radiophone."

"First let's have Bob's story. We haven't heard that yet," Mr. Crowninshield said. "Tell us what happened to you in New York, my boy."

Bob dropped into a chair.

"Well, as I wired you, Dacie and Lyman have landed your men. I recognized the fellow who came to Seaver Bay for water the instant I set eyes on him. He recognized me, too, and knew the game was up. It seems, though, that he and his pal are wanted in California on a prior charge. A big burglary, I think it is. Anyway, they have got to be taken out there and tried first. In the meantime our complaint can be lodged against them and——"

"Aren't we to have the fun of jailing them after all?" asked Dick in dismay.

"They will be jailed, never fear," returned Bob. "They will get a stiff sentence, too, I imagine."

Mr. Crowninshield was silent and his wife now glanced toward him.

"Are you disappointed, Archibald?" inquired she.

"I guess," responded he slowly, "that is a good way out of our dilemma. The villains will be carried far away from this vicinity and will without doubt get all that's coming to them. What more can we ask? We've won the game—taken every trick and made a clean sweep of the whole business. Now that

I've got Lola home I don't much care about the rest of it. What do you say we let well enough alone and drop it?"

"I should say that with every day of your life you were growing wiser, my dear," answered his wife softly.